Charlie Joe Jackson's Guide to Not Growing Hair

That makes absolutely no sense.

Nobody would want that guide!

By **Tommy Greenwald**

Pete Milano's Guide to Being a Movie Star
Katie Friedman Gives Up Texting!
(And Lives to Tell About It)
Jack Strong Takes a Stand

The **Charlie Joe Jackson Series**

Tommy Greenwald

Charlie Joe Jackson's Guide to

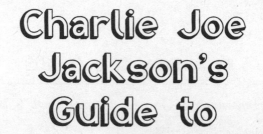

N**⊘**T

Now that's more like it!

Growing Up

Illustrations by J.P. Coovert

SQUARE
FISH

Roaring Brook Press ✳ New York

SQUARE
FISH

An imprint of Macmillan Publishing Group, LLC
175 Fifth Avenue
New York, NY 10010
mackids.com

Our books may be purchased in bulk for promotional, educational, or business use. Please
contact your local bookseller or the Macmillan Corporate and Premium Sales Department at
(800) 221-7945 ext. 5442 or by e-mail at MacmillanSpecialMarkets@macmillan.com.

Library of Congress Cataloging-in-Publication Data

Names: Greenwald, Tom, author. | Coovert, J. P., illustrator.
Title: Charlie Joe Jackson's guide to not growing up / Tommy Greenwald ; illustrated by J.P. Coovert.
Description: New York : Roaring Brook Press, 2016. | Series: Charlie Joe Jackson series ; 6 | Summary:
"As graduation day approaches, Charlie Joe is starting to realize being a kid isn't so bad after all"—
Provided by publisher.
Identifiers: LCCN 2015035808 | ISBN 9781250158352 (paperback) | ISBN 9781626721708 (ebook)
Subjects: | CYAC: Graduation (School)—Fiction. | Middle schools—Fiction. | Schools—Fiction. | Humorous
stories. | BISAC: JUVENILE FICTION / Humorous Stories. | JUVENILE FICTION / Social Issues /
Friendship.
Classification: LCC PZ7.G8523 Cgs 2016 | DDC [Fic]—dc23
LC record available at http://lccn.loc.gov/2015035808

Originally published in the United States by Roaring Brook Press
First Square Fish edition, 2018
Book designed by Andrew Arnold
Square Fish logo designed by Filomena Tuosto

10 9 8 7 6 5 4 3 2 1

AR: 4.3

For the nonreaders
who became readers

Youth is wasted on the young.
—George Bernard Shaw

I disagree.
—Charlie Joe Jackson

INTRODUCTION

My name is Charlie Joe Jackson, and I used to hate reading.

Guess what? Now I hate it a little less. (Let's keep that between us.)

I guess that's what they call part of "the maturing process."

Which brings us to the topic of this book.

Growing up.

I used to be all for it. I used to think the idea of being an adult was totally awesome—I could drive a car, and play video games whenever I wanted, and watch movies that my parents won't let me watch now.

But then one day I realized—that's *crazy*. What was I thinking?

And when I say "one day," I mean, one actual day.

The day I realized that being a kid was the best job in the world.

The day I decided to *not* grow up.

I had to act fast, because it was already happening. I was getting older, and I was about to lose the most carefree part of my life. Forever!

You don't have to tell me it was a crazy idea, I know

that already. Childhood is fleeting, nothing lasts forever—blah blah blah. Trying to stop time is impossible, right?

Wrong.

When it came to growing up, I wasn't going down without a fight.

✳ ✳ ✳

So anyway, not like I'm making excuses or anything, but hopefully that helps explain why, at exactly 5:51 on a lovely spring evening, there was a graduation ceremony happening at Eastport Middle School, with 183 students scheduled to graduate, but only 182 of them were present.

Want to guess who was missing?

Yup. You got it. Me.

Instead, there I was, sitting in a dark room by myself, wondering what the heck happened—and if it was somehow my fault, as usual.

There was a knock on the door.

"Charlie Joe? Are you in there?"

I closed my eyes and sighed. I wasn't exactly in the mood to see anybody right at that moment.

Oh, yeah—one more thing I forgot to mention.

It was my birthday.

Part One

LET'S GO BACK
TO THE BEGINNING,
SHALL WE?

8:49 am

"Yes!" I said to myself, as my eyes opened for the first time that morning.

Which, I can honestly say, had never happened before. Usually, the first words I say when I wake up are "Go away," and it comes out sounding more like "Murfleblorg."

But this was a morning different from any other. This, people, was a morning that I had been looking forward to ever since my mother first dragged me kicking and screaming to the school bus way back when. (I think you can still see the skid marks from my shoes at the bus stop.)

First of all, like I said, it was my birthday. Already a reason to celebrate, right?

But there was more—much, much more. Because this was the morning of the day I was graduating from Eastport Middle School. The first day of the rest of my life. The day I put the past behind me—all my crazy behavior and silly ideas and goofy troublemaking ways—and started acting like a mature person.

Or not.

I flipped over on the bed and reached for my phone, which was charging on the nightstand. I liked to sleep with my phone close by, and by close by, I mean approximately three inches away.

I texted my friend group—which included Timmy, Jake, Pete, and Nareem—two simple words: Today! Yeah!

Timmy texted back: See you at Jakes noon.

Nareem texted back: Very much looking forward to it.

Pete texted back: Rockin' high school baby.

Jake texted back: If you guys break anything in my house i'll kill you.

I was about to settle in for a nice long text war when there was a soft knock on the door.

"Honey?"

My mom poked her head in. She had a big blue balloon in her hand.

"Oh, hey, Mom," I said, putting my phone away. I didn't need her to start in with the you're-on-that-thing-too-much speech. There would be plenty of time for that later in the day. And for the rest of my life.

She kissed me on the cheek. "Happy birthday! Can you believe it? A birthday and a graduation all in one day!"

"Totally!" I said. "Although I do feel like I'm kind of getting ripped off. It would be nice to spread them out a little bit."

"I get that," Mom said.

I sat up in bed. "But, yeah, this is basically the best day of my life. No more middle school!"

"I thought you liked middle school."

"I guess so," I said, shrugging. Sometimes it's hard to explain to parents that you can like something but still want to never do it again. Sure, middle school *was* fun, but by the end, enough was enough, right? Time to move on.

"I better get going," I added, stretching. "Lots to do." But my mom wasn't moving. She was just sitting there, on the edge of my bed. This was weird—usually she had to beg me just to get up.

"Mom?"

"Yes, honey?"

"Like I said, I think I should probably get up."

She sighed. "It all goes by so fast."

"What does?"

"All of it." Then she took a tissue out of her pocket and blew her nose, which was also weird, since she never has a runny nose. "Megan's about to go to college. You're going off to high school. And you were both born yesterday."

"Yesterday?"

She smacked me on the head with a pillow. "Not literally yesterday," she said. "You're too young to get it, but time . . . you blink and the years fly by, just like that."

That was when I realized that my mom was blowing her nose because she was crying a little bit.

"Don't be sad!" I said. "I'm not going anywhere! And neither is Megan! We love home! Home is awesome!"

"I know, sweetheart." She smiled, but it seemed like part of the smile wasn't actually there. "It's just that these big milestone days, they're not easy on a mother. It was hard your first day of kindergarten, and it's hard now." She wiped her eyes one last time, then got up and went to the door. "See you downstairs, birthday-graduation boy."

After she left my room, I decided to close my eyes for just a few more minutes. I couldn't believe my mom was talking as if my first day of kindergarten had just happened. I could barely remember it at all . . .

"MOM! I CAN'T FIND MY LEFT SNEAKER!"

Young Charlie Joe Jackson was already late for his first day of kindergarten.

He stormed into the kitchen.

"I'M NOT GOING WITHOUT MY LEFT SNEAKER!"

"It was just in your room," his mother said, shaking her head. She knew what the real problem was. She knew he didn't want to go to school at all.

Together, they marched up to his room.

"SEE?" he announced. "IT'S NOT HERE!"

Without a word, his mother walked over to the closet, moved the toys, picked up the clothes, kicked away the balls, reached down, and pulled out a single blue shoe.

"Well what do you know?" she said. "Here it is."

Charlie Joe took one look at the shoe and burst out crying. "I CAN'T FIND MY FAVORITE SOCKS!"

After ten more minutes of crying, whining, and trying to make almost everything he owned disappear,

Charlie Joe Jackson reluctantly walked with his mother and father to the bus stop.

"Are you coming with me to school?" he asked.

"No," they said.

"WHY NOT?!" he asked.

"Because school is only for children," his mother said.

At the bus stop, several other children were also waiting, including Charlie Joe's neighbor, Timmy McGibney. Charlie Joe and Timmy didn't know each other very well, and they didn't like each other very much. Charlie Joe thought Timmy was irritating. Timmy thought Charlie Joe was annoying.

"Say hello to Timmy," Mrs. Jackson told Charlie Joe.

"Hello," said Charlie Joe—but he said it to the ground, not to Timmy.

"Say hello to Charlie Joe," said Timmy's mother.

Timmy just grunted.

The bus came, and a lady got out. She had a vest that said BUS MONITOR on it.

"Okay, kids, this is it!" she announced. "Time to make it happen! This is going to be the most fun day ever!"

Charlie Joe burst into tears.

"I'M NOT GOING! I HATE SCHOOL!"

His parents gently guided him toward the bus, but he wasn't making it easy for them.

All the other kids turned and watched. So did all the other parents, even though they pretended not to.

"SCHOOL IS FULL OF BOOKS AND OTHER TERRIBLE THINGS!" wailed Charlie Joe.

Finally, after much pulling, pushing, begging, and promising of after-school ice cream treats, Charlie Joe got on the bus.

"I just want you both to know that I will never forgive you," he told his parents.

A single tear ran down his mom's cheek as the bus drove away, while his dad kept waving long after the bus had drifted out of sight.

Finally, Charlie Joe's parents looked at each other.

"I thought that went well," his dad said.

9:12 am

I was still lying in bed when I heard eight legs charging down the hall.

"Moose! Coco!"

My two favorite people in the whole world—even though they're not technically people—rounded the corner into my room.

"Get up!" they said with their tails. "Get up now!"

So I did, kind of. I got up, but then I fell down onto the floor and let them jump on top of me like they did every morning.

It's the best way to wake up, by the way. I highly recommend it.

After two minutes, though, I noticed that Moose was watching more than playing. He'd been doing that a lot lately.

"You are so lazy," I told him. He answered me with a single thump of his huge tail. He knew that I knew he wasn't lazy. Moose was just getting old. It happens young with dogs.

"Let's go downstairs, you guys," I told them, and they

followed me into the kitchen. My sister, Megan, was already there, scarfing down her breakfast. You know how you hear about those girls who are obsessed with their weight and don't eat enough? Megan wasn't one of those girls.

"Jeez, save some for the rest of the country," I told her.

Her answer was to open her mouth wide, revealing a soggy mountain of partially chewed scrambled eggs.

I gagged. "Eeeew!"

She opened her mouth wider. "Happy birthday, baby brother!"

"You are beyond gross!"

"You are beyond annoying!"

My mom immediately went into peacemaker mode, which she actually didn't have to do all that often, because believe it or not, I really like my older sister. "Honey, I'm making your birthday breakfast specialty," my mom said.

I felt my mouth start to twitch. "Wait. Chocolate chip pancakes?"

"Yup."

"Sweeeeet!" I poured myself a glass of milk to get ready.

My mom sipped her coffee. "Megan was just telling me about her summer job."

Ack! Summer job? That sounds like one of those oxymorons teachers keep telling us about. Like jumbo shrimp. Or good book.

"What kind of job?" I asked.

I waited while Megan took a ten-second swig of orange juice. "I'm working at the yoga place as a babysitter."

I snorted. "Oh. I thought by job, you meant, like, actual *job*. As opposed to lying on a couch texting your friends while some kiddies watch *Sesame Street*."

Megan was about to throw a piece of toast at me, but my mom stopped her. "That's not fair, Charlie Joe, and you know it," Mom said. "Looking after children is very hard work." She shot me a look. "I should know."

"Yeah," said Megan. "And what about you? You're graduating middle school; that means soon you'll be old enough to get a job, too, so watch it."

"Never!" I said. "I'm never going to have a summer job. And if I do, it will be at a summer camp, teaching napping."

"Well, you're very good at that," my mom agreed.

The oven dinged.

"Ah, the muffins," said my mom. "Charlie Joe, I'm going to need you to bring these across the street to the new neighbor."

Noooo! First I had to deal with talk of a summer job, and now I'm supposed to bring muffins to some strange old man who just moved in across the street?

"On my birthday? Why?"

"Because it's the nice thing to do, that's why."

I rolled my eyes. "Mom, why do you have to be so nice all the time?" I whined. "The rest of us have to pay the price."

"Come on, it's not going to kill you," she said. "He seems very friendly. Someone told me he's a writer."

"Now Charlie Joe is definitely not going," Megan said, between forkfuls.

"Can I bring the dogs?" I asked.

"No, you can't bring the dogs," answered my mom. "Stop asking if you can bring the dogs everywhere you go. Normal people don't do that."

"Dad does," I reminded her.

"My point exactly," she said.

10:18 am

The house across the street used to be occupied by the Kellys. Audrey Kelly, who was a few years older than Megan, wanted to be an actress. Actually, it was her mom, Eileen, who *really* wanted Audrey to be an actress. They decided to move to New York City to be closer to all the agents and people like that. On the day they left, we were waving goodbye when my dad said to my mom, "Should we tell them that Audrey has no talent?" My mom thought for a second and said, "It might be a little too late for that."

They ended up selling the house to this older guy. I'd only seen him once, through a window, watching a giant TV. But now, here I was, ringing his doorbell with a plate of muffins in my hand.

The door opened. The man looked even older in person. "Yes?"

"Uh, hello, sir. My name is Charlie Joe Jackson. We live across the street. My mother made muffins for you."

The man peered at me through thick glasses. For a second, I thought he was going to tell me to scram, because

17

you always think that old people are going to tell you to scram. But instead, he broke out into a big smile.

"Well, that's mighty kind of your mom," he said. "My name's Ted. Would you like to come in for a short minute?"

I had to decide whether to be honest or be polite. "Uh, okay, sure," I said. My mother would have been proud. But she wasn't even there to see it. What a waste.

We went into Ted's kitchen, where he poured me a glass of juice. "Seems like a fine neighborhood," he said.

"Yeah, it's great." I took a sip. "Do you have kids or anything? I mean, most people who live around here have kids."

Ted sat down next to me with an old-man sigh. "Well, yes I do, but they're older," he said. "In fact, they have kids of their own. That's the whole reason I bought this house. It's nice and small, so I can manage it, but I've also got a yard, and a neighborhood full of kids, for when my grandchildren come visit."

I nodded. "That makes sense. All I know is, my parents are glad you moved in, because they were really worried someone was going to tear this house down and build one of those ridiculously huge, gross mansions."

"Not me." Ted chuckled. He got up and brought a bowl of grapes over to the table. We each helped ourselves. "So tell me, young man, how old are you?"

My phone buzzed. "Sorry," I said to Ted, as I checked it.

"Quite all right," he said, laughing softly. "I'm used to it."

It was a text from Katie Friedman: `just found out, no swimming today at Jake's party!` I texted back: `It's all Jake's mom's fault.`

I put my phone away. "That was my girlfriend, Katie." I still felt a little proud whenever I said that, even though we'd been going out for a while. "We're going to a barbecue later at my friend's house to celebrate graduating from middle school."

"Middle school!" said Ted, clapping his hands together. "Wow."

"I know, I can't wait," I said.

Ted frowned. "You can't wait for what?"

"To graduate," I explained. "To go to high school. I mean, I'm a little nervous I guess, but it's going to be so cool being with the older kids!"

Ted took a sip of his juice, which was purple and smelled like something an old person might drink. "Let me tell you something, young man. I would give anything— and I mean *anything*—to be back in middle school again. To be so young, without a care in the world, just having fun and trying to learn a few things along the way—now that's what I call perfection."

"Yeah, but—" I hesitated, reluctant to call an old man by his first name.

"Ted," he said, reading my mind.

I exhaled. "Yeah, but Ted, can't you always have fun, no matter how old you are? I feel like the thing is, at a certain point you grow out of middle school."

"You're right," said Ted. "At a certain point you *do* grow out of middle school." He popped the last grape into his mouth. "And therein lies the pity. We all grow out, and we all grow up."

I scratched my head. "There*what* lies the *what*? And what's wrong with growing up?"

Ted suddenly jumped up with the speed of someone approximately fifty-five years younger. "What was your name again, son?"

"Charlie Joe."

"Well, Charlie Joe, do you know something? I'm a writer. In fact, I'm a writer of books for people just like you. Do you like to read?"

I hesitated. Wow, that was a loaded question. Reading and I have a long, checkered history.

"It's complicated," I said.

"Well, I have something for you," Ted said, bounding into another room. "Let's call it a graduation present!"

"What is it?" I called back, smiling at the thought of a sweet DVD collection, or maybe a new video game that just came on the market.

"A book!" sang out Ted.

ACK!

"A what?"

"A book! It's one of my favorites, but I can't seem to find it right now. Give me one sec."

By the time he said "Give me one sec," though, I was already halfway to the front door.

"Uh, yeah, Ted? Um, I just remembered that I have this thing that I need to go to."

Ted reappeared in the hallway. "Thing?"

I shuffled my feet. "Yeah. A graduation-type thing."

"Of course." Ted opened the door. "That will give me time to dig it up. I can give it to you later, since it's entirely possible I'll see you later on today."

I scratched my head. "You will?"

He smiled mysteriously. "Quite possibly, yes."

"Oh, okay, great." He stuck out his hand, and after a second I realized he wanted me to shake it, so I did. "Well, good to meet you, Ted. And, uh, thanks for the juice."

"Anytime, young man. And thank your mom for these wonderful muffins!"

As I walked back home, I felt a little bad. I didn't have the heart to tell Ted the truth—that the only other time I'd ever been given books as a present, it qualified as one of the worst days of my life.

No, scratch that.

The worst.

FLASHBACK!!

"HEY! IT'S MY BIRTHDAY!" screamed young Charlie Joe Jackson, for approximately the 427th time in three hours.

Charlie Joe knew that everybody was tired of him yelling that, but he didn't care. It was the best day of the whole year, and he wanted everyone to know it. He was finally, finally, FINALLY six years old. It seemed like he had been five and three-quarters forever!

Birthdays were great because you got to do whatever you wanted.

You were allowed to watch a ton of TV.

You were allowed to have ice cream for breakfast.

You were allowed to tell your older sister to BUZZ OFF!

But mainly, Charlie Joe loved his birthday for the same reason most people love birthdays.

PRESENTS.

"What am I gonna get?" Charlie Joe asked his parents, all day long. "And when am I gonna get it?"

"Soon," they kept saying. "At the party."

Finally, it was time. Mom and Dad were home

from work, his sister, Megan, was done with soccer practice, and all of his classmates from school were gathered in the kitchen.

"I'M READY!" Charlie Joe announced.

"That's good, because I couldn't tell," said Charlie Joe's dad. He always made sarcastic comments like that.

Megan turned out the lights, and Mom lit the candles on the chocolate coconut cake that was Charlie Joe's favorite.

"Happy birthday to you . . ." everyone sang. But Charlie Joe couldn't wait for the end of the song. He blew out the candles on the word dear and had already finished his first piece by the word Joe.

"Easy there, champ," said Charlie Joe's dad.

"But it's really good cake," Charlie Joe answered, although his mouth was full, so it sounded more like "Bufireelguhkafe."

After two quick slices, Charlie Joe made sure his mom wasn't looking, then wiped his mouth on his shirt. He placed himself at the head of the table, because that was where the present receiver always sat.

"I'm ready," he announced. Then he opened all the gifts from the other kids. There were some nice things, like a video game and a sweatshirt, but all he really wanted to do was open the presents from his family. They always got him the best and biggest things.

"Can I open my presents now?" he asked his parents.

His dad clapped his hands together. "Okay! But first, you have to close your eyes." Charlie Joe shut them tight, dreaming of all sorts of possibilities: A trampoline? A bicycle? A giant teddy bear made out of chocolate and marshmallows? A—

"Okay, let 'er rip!" announced his dad.

Charlie Joe opened his eyes and saw a giant gift sitting on the table. It was as tall as tall can be. That was a good sign! Big presents were the best kind of presents!

"Now, Charlie Joe—" began his mom, but she was too late. He was already tearing into the present the same way a starving dog tears into a steak.

Down went the bow. Off came the ribbons. RIP! went the wrapping paper, which went flying all over the kitchen.

At last, the present was revealed. Charlie Joe stared at it, looking completely shocked. And not in a good way.

There, before him, stood a pile of books a mile high.

Tears immediately sprung to his six-year-old eyes. "Wait . . . what?"

"It's the collected works of Mark Twain," said his mom.

"We thought it was a good time for you to discover the wonder of reading," said his dad.

His sister immediately started laughing. "Hahahahahahahahaha!" she said.

"This is my PRESENT?" Charlie Joe said, his voice rising higher with each word. "BOOKS? BOOKS ARE MY PRESENT?"

Charlie Joe's mother realized that things were quickly going wrong. "Well, yes, Charlie Joe, but we also got you a few other things." She produced another gift from behind her back. Charlie Joe ripped it open. It was a baseball glove.

"I hate baseball," he said, even though that wasn't true. He threw the glove on the floor, which made it official. Charlie Joe's birthday was ruined.

"Maybe we should go," said one of the other moms.

"No way," said Timmy McGibney, the boy from next door, who was watching Charlie Joe's meltdown with immense enjoyment.

Charlie Joe's father tried to calm down his son. "Charlie Joe, sooner or later you're going to have to start reading," he said. "Mark Twain is one of our most wonderful writers. He's a national treasure. And he's hilarious, too!"

"I HATE MARK TWAIN!" Charlie Joe hollered. "AND I HATE READING! AND I HATE EVERYTHING!"

Then he knocked the books off the table onto the floor. The noise scared his puppy, Moose, who ran to the far end of the house.

"Sorry, Moose," Charlie Joe said, through his sniffles.

His parents had seen enough. "Charlie Joe!" snapped his dad. "I don't care if it is your birthday—you need to take a break for a few minutes."

"I WILL!"

Charlie Joe ran upstairs, slammed the door, and cried into his pillow. A little while later, his mother knocked on the door.

"Are you ready to come back to the party?" she asked. "It's still your birthday, last I checked. And all your friends are going to leave soon, so you need to say goodbye to them and thank them for coming."

Charlie Joe rubbed his eyes and didn't say anything. But he got up out of bed and went downstairs. The first thing he did was find another piece of cake.

"Bye-everyone-thank-you-for-coming," he said, with absolutely no graciousness whatsoever.

"Charlie Joe, I'm sorry you're so disappointed," said his dad. "But you need to apologize to your friends, for behaving so badly."

"I'm sorry," Charlie Joe said, with absolutely no remorse whatsoever.

"That's okay," said an adorable little girl named Eliza, who was batting her eyelashes lovingly at Charlie Joe.

Charlie Joe looked around and noticed something—the Mark Twain collection was nowhere in sight.

"What happened to all the books?" he asked.

"We gave them to this little boy right here," said Charlie Joe's mom, pointing at a shy boy with glasses. Charlie Joe didn't even know the boy's name and had barely ever spoken to him before.

Charlie Joe looked at the boy. "Who are you again?"

The little boy adjusted his glasses. "Jake," he said. "Jake Katz."

"He loves to read!" said some annoying woman, who was probably Jake's mother.

"I don't," Charlie Joe replied, as if everyone didn't know that already.

Charlie Joe ate his cake and stared at Jake, with one thing going through his mind: I WILL NEVER BE FRIENDS WITH THIS KID.

_12:12 pm_

Jake Katz is one of my best friends,

but that doesn't mean I have to be best friends with his mom.

She's a little crazy, and not in the good, Pete Milano kind of way. She's crazy in the my-child-is-better-than-your-child-and-I'm-going-to-make-sure-everyone-knows-it kind of way.

"Welcome to our home!" Mrs. Katz sang out, as my parents and I walked into their house for the pre-graduation barbecue. "Charlie Joe, please feel free to join the other children."

What's the cut-off age for when adults stop calling you "children," anyway?

My dad tried not to sigh, as he prepared himself for a conversation with Mrs. Katz. Meanwhile, I veered off toward the kitchen, so I could make a quick pit stop. The good news was that the Katz's fridge always had a ton of delicious treats inside. The bad news was that to access them, you had to read everything that was plastered on the door:

29

Jake's report card—straight A's.

Jake's various certificates and awards for being a genius.

Jake's sister Sara's Merit Scholarship letter.

Jake's dog Elmer's Certificate of Good Behavior from the Wag-a-rama Obedience School.

Do I need to go on, or do you get my point?

Nevertheless, it was a small price to pay for the Fudgsicle I helped myself to, before heading out to join my friends.

"Charlie Joe!" hollered Jake, from the Ping-Pong table. He was playing with Nareem. They were both obsessed with Ping-Pong. It's the perfect sport for people who don't play sports.

"Hey!" I hollered back, but I didn't walk over. I didn't want to interrupt the game, and besides, there was someone else I was looking for.

I found her sitting at a picnic table with a bunch of other girls. Nearby, the pool just sat there, sad and lonely, wondering why no one was swimming in it.

"Hey, Katie," I said. "I brought you a Fudgsicle."

She looked up and smiled. "You're so sweet!"

"We're in the middle of an important conversation," said Eliza Collins, who was sitting next to Katie. Eliza wasn't all that happy that Katie and I were going out. She'd always kind of liked me, even though she showed it mostly by being mean to me whenever she could.

"Okay." I started to walk away, but then I heard a voice behind me.

"Wait!"

I turned around and saw Hannah Spivero. Hannah used to be the girl of my dreams for about seven years, but then she started going out with Jake Katz, which turned my dreams into nightmares, until I met Zoe Alvarez, who was my almost-girlfriend until she moved away, which is when I realized I'd always really liked Katie Friedman, who unfortunately had just broken up with my good friend Nareem Ramdal at the time, which made things pretty awkward for a while.

I know it sounds really complicated, but it's not. It's just middle school.

"Hey, Hannah."

She pulled my arm. "Come talk to me for a second."

We veered over by the soda table, where I grabbed a root beer. "What's up?"

"It's time," she said, as if I was supposed to know exactly what she was talking about. I didn't.

"What's time?"

She leaned in, her lips only about four inches from my ear. There was a time not that long ago where her being that close to me would have made me sweat, stammer, and possibly pass out. But that was then. Things were completely different now.

"Jake," she said, mysteriously.

"W-what about him?" Okay fine, I stammered a bit. Old habits die hard.

"You need to tell him something for me. Something he's not going to like."

Wait a second. Was she saying what I think she was saying?

My head went a little fuzzy. You have to understand—entire school years went by while I daydreamed about hearing those words. But like I said—that was then, and this is now.

"What?" I asked. "What do you need me to tell him?"

"Shhhh!" she whispered, way too loudly to be considered an actual whisper. "I don't want to do anything about it until after graduation!"

"Sorry, but this doesn't make any sense."

Hannah twirled a straw around in her mouth. "We're about to go to high school, and we're going to meet a whole bunch of new kids, and it just seems like the right time, like it makes sense, you know?"

"No!" I objected, probably a little too loudly. "You're like, the best couple in the school, not counting Phil and

Celia." I was referring to Phil Manning and Celia Barbarossa, who'd been going out for so long people were starting to call them Philarossa. I swigged my soda, then refilled. "Plus, I just don't think you should break up with him today of all days. That would be terrible."

Hannah burst out laughing.

"Break up with him? What??"

I felt my face start to turn red. "Why, what were you talking about?"

"I just was going to say Jake needs to think about maybe getting contact lenses, that's all!" Hannah said, between gasps of laughter. "And start dressing better."

"Oh," I said.

She wiped her eyes. "That's like, totally hilarious that you thought I wanted to break up with him! Oh my God! No, it's just that it's high school, you know, and he needs to look good, and grow up a little bit, that's all I'm saying."

I suddenly got a little annoyed. "Why is everyone all obsessed about the future, and what's next, and growing up all of a sudden? I'm starting to get sick of it. What's wrong with right now?" I polished off my second glass of root beer. "Man, this is turning into a lousy birthday."

Hannah's eyes went wide. "Oh my gosh! Your birthday! I totally forgot!" She turned around and shouted, "Everybody! It's Charlie Joe's birthday!!"

Well, that did it. Everyone came running over and

started pounding me on the back, shouting "Way to go!" and "Congratulations, Charlie Joe! You're the man!" But I didn't exactly feel like the man, right then. I felt a little confused, to tell you the truth.

Jake came over and put his arm around Hannah. She glanced quickly at me, then smiled at Jake—and I noticed Jake was starting to sprout a little mustache.

Yup, middle school was definitely over.

Pete Milano came over and put me in a headlock. "Happy birthday, Charlie Joe! Here's my present!" He threw in a couple of noogies for good measure.

"Uh, Pete?" I gasped. "That kind of hurts."

"Birthdays are supposed to hurt," he said, but then he let me go.

I tried to catch my breath. "What's up?"

"Oh you know, dude, the usual," Pete said. "This party's a little lame."

"What do you mean?" I said.

"I mean, this party's a little lame," Pete repeated. In the old days, I would have rolled my eyes at Pete, who used to be even more of a troublemaker than I was. But that was before he starred in a big Hollywood movie and became the coolest kid in school.

"Yeah, I guess you're right," I said.

Pete adjusted his sunglasses. He wore them all the time, because he thought they made him look sophisticated. I thought they just made him look goofy, which I'm allowed to say, because they were a gift from my friends and me.

"Aren't we old enough yet so the adults don't have to be at all our parties, keeping an eye on us?" Pete asked. "I mean, what's the deal with that?" He shrugged. "Anyway, I gotta go find Mareli, before she finds me." Mareli was Pete's girlfriend, and she liked to know where he was at all times.

"Okay, see you later." I looked over at the parents, who were up on the porch mingling. They were all wearing nice shirts, and skirts, and colorful shorts. Half of them were staring at their phones. Didn't any of them want to jump in the pool? Didn't any of them want to splash around like an idiot? Didn't any of them want to . . . you know . . . act like a kid?

All of a sudden, I found myself taking my shirt and shoes off, then running full speed toward the pool.

"Cannonball!" I shouted, launching myself into the air.

I balled up and jumped as high as I could, for maximum impact.

SPLASH!

By the time I came up to the surface, three girls were screaming because I'd gotten them all wet, and three boys had jumped into the pool after me. One of them was Timmy McGibney, who always tried to do what I did, only bigger and louder.

"Let's do this!" he screamed, jumping around and splashing everyone in sight.

"Last one to the other side is a rotten egg!" I hollered.

"Go!" he yelled.

It was a close race—and when I looked up, the first thing I saw was Jake's mom, standing over us.

"Boys! Boys! I said no swimming! You all have a big day ahead of you! Please, everyone out now!"

"Sorry, Mrs. Katz," said Eric Cunkler, one of the other boys who'd jumped in.

Timmy and I looked at each other, trying to decide what to do. For a minute I thought about doing about five more cannonballs, but then I saw my parents looking at me, and I realized that nothing good could come from it.

"Be right out, Mrs. Katz," I said. "It's just that the water is so nice."

Mrs. Katz was in the middle of flashing me her best fake smile when I heard an oddly familiar voice scream "COMING THROUGH!" Then, all of a sudden, a kid came flying past all the adults, past the catering people putting out lunch, and past the kids already sitting at the picnic tables. The kid was moving so fast I couldn't tell who it was, but he took a flying leap into the pool, flailing his arms like a spastic baboon. He hit the water with a

THWACK! that sounded like the worst belly flop in the history of belly flops. *Ouch*, I thought. Then I thought, *Who is this crazy kid?* And then I thought, *I'm so happy there's another moron here, so I'm not the only one.*

When the kid came to the surface, it all made sense.

Teddy Spivero.

No way!

"Hey, Wacko Jacko!" he gasped, water still coming out of his nose. "Long time no sneeze!"

Way.

"What's up, Teddy?" I said, trying to sound perfectly normal and friendly. See, here's the thing: Teddy Spivero was my archenemy ever since I first knew what the word *archenemy* meant. He was Hannah's twin brother, and I'd spent approximately half my life trying to figure out how a perfect girl and a horrible boy could have the same exact genetic makeup. (A phrase I learned in eighth-grade science.)

Teddy promptly swam down to the shallow end of the pool, where I was hanging out, and splashed about a gallon of water directly into my mouth.

"What did you do that for?!?" I sputtered.

"Because it was fun!" was his answer.

And you know something? I couldn't argue with his logic. From his perspective, it probably *was* fun. Which was something this barbecue could've used a lot more of, right about then.

37

Teddy was clearly thinking the same thing. "What kind of party is this?" he said. "It's like somebody died or something!"

"We're not supposed to be swimming," I told him. "Mrs. Katz said."

"That's major lame," Teddy said.

"We're going to get in trouble if we don't get out," I said, hating myself for being so . . . well, lame.

"Oh, no!" he yelled, splashing me again. *The heck with it*, I thought, and splashed him back. Which led to a fairly significant water war. It got so splashy that Timmy swam over.

"Mrs. Katz is going to kill you guys!"

"Kill us why?" asked Teddy. "Because we're actually playing with water in a swimming pool?"

That might have been the moment I decided I kind of liked Teddy Spivero.

"Kids, out!" hollered Mrs. Katz. "I mean it! It's time for lunch anyway!"

"But it's just so darn nice in here!" Teddy hollered back. "Can we swim while we eat?" I was starting to like him more and more.

"This is simply a modest way to kick off the day," Mrs. Katz told us, as if we cared. "After lunch, everyone needs to go home and get ready for the afternoon festivities."

"I don't know about you," Teddy whispered to me, "but

I can get ready in about eight seconds flat." I decided the best thing to do at that moment was to ignore him.

The good news was, Mrs. Katz takes her food very, *very* seriously. After Timmy and I hopped out and dried ourselves off, we checked out the picnic tables, which were filled with hot dogs, cheeseburgers, every kind of chip ever invented, cookies, brownies, cupcakes, and approximately fourteen different kinds of soda.

"Mamma Mia, this looks delicious," Timmy said.

For some reason, though, no one was eating yet. I couldn't figure out why, until Mrs. Katz started clinking a glass. "Please, everyone, gather around for a quick toast!" she called.

Oh jeez.

The adults came down from the screen porch, and the kids came up from the lawn. Katie came over to me and we joined a big circle. Jake's mom stood right in the middle of everyone, which was exactly the way she wanted it.

"I'd like to congratulate all of the young men and women who are here today," she began.

Oh, so all of a sudden we're men and women?

"Tonight you become graduates of Eastport Middle School and get ready for the next step at high school," she continued. "I'm just so proud of all of you, including my young Jake, who has had such a marvelous experience at school, with all his friends, having fun learning, and soaking in so much knowledge. It's really been wonderful to watch."

I glanced over at Jake. He looked like he wanted to crawl into a hole.

"I thought it might be nice to have a moment of reflection on this day of celebration," Mrs. Katz continued. "We've all been through so much, and you kids are just so terrific. You've worked so hard and kept your heads on straight. So here's to all of you!"

Everyone said some variation of "Cheers!" or "Yay!"

"That wasn't so bad," I whispered to Katie.

"It's not over," she whispered back.

"How do you know?"

"Trust me."

Sure enough, Mrs. Katz kept her glass of whatever it was in the air. "And now," she said, "I'd like for us to go around and ask each child what you're looking forward to most about high school. Perhaps it's a subject you'd like to take, or a teacher you've heard is very good, or a sport you're going to play, or a club you plan on joining. Because today is as much about looking forward to the future as it is celebrating the past." She looked around the lawn. "Who wants to go first?"

Shockingly enough, no one wanted to go first. As kids shuffled their feet and tried to avoid eye contact with Jake's mom, I glanced at my dad. He saw me, then laughed and

shrugged, as if to say, *This is your problem, pal, not mine.*
He was right.

As the uncomfortable silence got longer, Mrs. Katz's eyes started to take on a slightly desperate shine. "Jake, why don't you start us off?"

Poor Jake looked as if he knew that was coming. "Uh, okay, sure . . . I guess if I had to say what I was looking forward to most, it would be maybe the debate team, which I heard was really fun."

Debate *team*? Huh—I had no idea debate was a sport. But okay, we can go with that if you want.

Phil Manning jumped in next. "I'm planning to play football and rugby, and maybe join the wrestling team," he said. "And hopefully, you know, study a lot and stuff." His girlfriend Celia Barbarossa was next to him—they're never more than seven inches apart—and she piped in, "I hope to join the model U.N."

"I'd like to take a bunch of AP courses," said some other kid that I barely knew.

"Me, too," murmured a bunch of other kids in agreement.

Teddy looked confused, then elbowed me in the ribs. "What's an AP course?"

I wasn't sure, either. "Uh—" I said, before Katie chimed in. "It's short for Advanced Placement," she said. "Kids who want to get into good colleges take them. They're really hard."

"Who cares?" said Teddy Spivero, at which point he officially went from my enemy to my friend. He elbowed me again. "Let's go inside and check out the house."

"Huh?" I had a sudden flashback to the last time I snuck away from someone giving a speech. It was at the New York Public Library during Camp Rituhbukkee Reunion Weekend, and it didn't end well at all.

"Come on!" Teddy urged. "This house is sweet. Let's give ourselves a tour."

"I've been inside lots of times," I told Teddy. He obviously thought that was a pretty weak argument, because he took off toward the house.

Meanwhile, Eliza Collins was raising her hand. "My goal is to become head cheerleader," she said, "while also starting a club that raises money for the endangered species of the world, such as the black-footed ferret."

That was all I needed to hear. I snuck out of the circle and caught up to Teddy just as he was opening the door of the screen porch.

"You know what my goal for high school is?" he said. "To not get arrested."

And with that, we entered the house.

12:51 pm

It turned out that I had nothing to worry about: Teddy wasn't interested in ransacking Jake's house and looking for valuable items to stuff down his pants.

Instead, he just wanted to park himself in the living room, gorge on Doritos, and talk about what a bunch of losers everyone in Eastport was.

"I don't know, man," he said. "The people here are just so wrapped up in like, being the best, and getting ahead, and doing better than the next guy. It's wack."

"Not everyone," I told Teddy. "Jake's mom is a little crazy for sure, but most people are pretty cool."

Teddy put his feet up on a table I'm pretty sure was not supposed to have feet on it. "Yeah, whatever you need to tell yourself. You heard those kids out there, right? They've all got a plan. Everybody has a plan. Everybody's in a hurry. What's the rush, I say? Why can't everyone just relax?" He picked a piece of dirt off his thigh and flicked it toward a garbage can. It missed by about five feet. "Well, Wacko Jacko? Am I right or what?"

"Today's my birthday," I said, which wasn't exactly the answer to his question.

"No way!" Teddy leaped out of his seat and came over to give me a never-ending noogie. "Happy birthday, dude!"

"Thanks," I said. "Should we go back outside?"

Teddy shook his head dramatically, his wet hair spraying water all over the room. "Not yet. Let's wait for a minute, to make sure that everyone had a chance to say what they're going to be awesome at in high school."

"That makes sense."

Teddy and I sat quietly for a minute.

"Man, these dudes got a lot of books," he said, staring at the wall.

"Yup," I said. He was stating the obvious—the whole room had bookshelves that stretched from floor to ceiling, and they were completely crammed. As I looked around, I realized I'd never sat in their living room before. I'd barely ever sat in *my* living room before. Which makes sense. As far as I know, absolutely no living of any kind is ever done in *anyone's* living room.

I was absent-mindedly looking around at the shelves when I suddenly saw a group of books that looked oddly familiar. The yellow covers . . . The red letters . . . Wait a second!

I got up to take a closer look.

Yup . . . that was them.

The Complete Works Of Mark Twain.

"Holy smokes," I said. "I can't believe it."

Teddy, who was picking his fingernails with his shoe-laces, looked up. "Can't believe what?"

"These used to be my books," I told him. "I got them for my sixth birthday. But I threw a massive tantrum because I thought it was a terrible present, and so my parents gave them to Jake."

I picked one up. *The Adventures of Tom Sawyer.* It looked like it had been read a zillion times.

"So they're your books?" Teddy asked.

"Not exactly. Not anymore, anyway."

He came over to the bookshelf and started running his finger over the books. "I was never much of a reader," he said.

I nodded. "I'm right there with you."

"But I still think it was wrong for your parents to give them away," Teddy said. "I mean, after all, what if some day you have kids of your own, and they turn into big readers, and you wanted to give them the books that were given to you when you were a kid?" He plucked one off the shelf and examined it. "They'd probably be worth a lot of money by then, too."

"I suppose."

Teddy turned and looked at me. "Let's take them back."

"Huh?"

He pointed his finger at the bookshelf and started counting. "What do we got, about ten books here? Let's take them back. They'll never know."

"What do you mean, they'll never know?" I took a quick glance into the kitchen, where the catering people were getting ready to bring out more food. "We can't just steal stuff. That's like, illegal."

"Okay, fine," Teddy said, clearly disappointed in my lack of criminality. "Then let's just move them somewhere."

I was confused. "Move them somewhere?"

"Yeah, like hide them."

"Huh? Hide them where? What for?"

"Look," Teddy said, pointing. "See how every book here is arranged by alphabetical order?" He was right. Mark Twain was right between William Styron (I had no idea who that was) and John Updike (ditto).

"So what? You think they'll care if a few books are out of place?"

Teddy snorted. "Have you met Mrs. Katz?"

I looked out the window and saw her rearranging the silverware on one of the picnic tables.

"I still don't get the point, though."

"Just to have a little fun," Teddy said, starting to pull the Twain books down from the shelf. "You remember fun, don't you? That thing we used to have, before everyone started thinking about annoying stuff, like the future?"

I thought about what Teddy said. What he wanted to do was stupid, silly, and pointless. But since when had that ever stopped me before?

"Okay, fine."

We started pulling the books down from the shelf, and we each had a bunch of books stuffed in our arms when I heard a soft little bark behind me. I turned around to see Elmer, the Katz's cockapoo, checking us out.

"Oh, hey Elmer," I said, suddenly feeling guilty. Elmer and I were good pals. What if he could tell what we were up to?

"Charlie Joe? Charlie Joe? CHARLIE JOE!"

"What?" I turned around to see Teddy standing there, white as a ghost. He pointed at Elmer, who was happily wagging his tail.

"What?" I said again.

"I . . . don't . . . like . . . dogs," stammered Teddy.

Translation: He was scared to death of them.

"Oh," I said. I was just about to say *cockapoos are the least scary-looking dogs in the whole world, and Elmer's the nicest dog ever, if you don't count Moose and Coco,* when Elmer suddenly decided he wanted to make friends with Teddy. Which meant, he gave out a playful *BARK!* and charged.

"AARGHH!" screamed Teddy, and without another word, he charged out the screen door with Elmer right behind him. I decided the only thing to do was to try and help

47

my friend—Teddy had technically only been my friend for about eight minutes at that point, but it still counted—and so I followed right behind. The three of us ran down the hill, past the lunch tables where everyone was still going through what they wanted to do in high school (I thought I heard Nareem say he was planning on joining the fish sticks club, but later I found out he'd said statistics club, which was too bad—I'd been all excited about the fish sticks club), across the volleyball court that had been set up, and straight toward the pool.

"Teddy wait!" I hollered, but I'm not sure he could hear me—Elmer, who thought we were playing a really fun game, was barking at the top of his doggie lungs.

SPLASH! went Teddy into the pool. Elmer was just about to dive in, but I managed to grab his collar first.

"Elmer, no!"
I said.

"Charlie Joe, yes!" he said back—or would have, if he could talk.

Then Elmer gave a yank—it turns out cockapoos are really strong, which I didn't realize until it was too late—and together we followed Teddy into the pool.

SPLASH!

SPLASH!

It wasn't until I was underwater and I saw a strange object float by me that I realized what had been in my hands this whole time—and no, I'm not talking about Elmer's collar.

I'm talking about Mark Twain's books.

I splashed to the surface and looked around the pool. Teddy had also leaped into the pool with books still in his hands. So all together, there were ten books, two kids, and one waterlogged cockapoo in the pool. The good news was, Elmer was no longer interested in Teddy. His new fun game was grabbing soggy books with his teeth and ripping them apart.

"Elmer, no!" I said again, with exactly the same non-result.

By this time, the splashing and thrashing had gotten the attention of the rest of the party, and everyone had come running over to see what all the commotion was about.

Mrs. Katz barged her way through to the front of the crowd. "May I ask what is going on here?"

I saw Jake next to her, scratching his head in confusion.

Hopefully he would think this whole thing was funny and realize it would make a great story to tell the debate team some day.

Mrs. Katz's eyes widened in horror. "Are those . . . *books?!*" she shrieked.

"I can explain," I began, which of course means, *I can't explain.*

Meanwhile, Teddy Spivero was down at the other end of the pool, thrilled that he wasn't about to be eaten by a rabid cockapoo. "Hey, Mrs. Katz," he said, waving. "This pool is so nice. Is it heated?"

"Yes, it's on an automatic timer," she answered. Even when she's really mad, Mrs. Katz doesn't like to miss an opportunity to throw in a quick brag.

"Sweet," answered Teddy. "It's like, the perfect place to chill."

Mrs. Katz looked like she'd just eaten a rotten banana. "Teddy, I'm going to have to ask you to exit the pool," she said. "You, too, Charlie Joe."

As we climbed out and dried off (for the second time), I saw some of the kids trying not to giggle. All succeeded except Pete Milano, who laughed and said, "Charlie Joe, I know you don't like reading, but drowning books seems a little extreme."

I laughed, looking down at the pages floating in the water. "Yeah, well, you can never be too careful."

That probably wasn't the smartest or nicest thing to say, considering the circumstances.

Jake came over to me, looking almost as mad as his mom. "So this is funny to you? Destroying my stuff? You might not care about books, Charlie Joe, but some of us do, you know. Some of us care a lot."

"It was an accident," I said. "Teddy and I were just inside, and I was showing him the books, and telling him the story of how we gave them to you on my sixth birthday." I was trying to accomplish a lot with that sentence: remind him that they were my books in the first place, and remind everyone else that it was my birthday.

I left out the part about Teddy's plan to annoy Jake's mom by putting them somewhere else. I'm not sure including that part would have accomplished anything at all.

Hannah, who was standing next to Jake, scrunched up her eyes. "An accident?" she said. "Running into the pool with a bunch of books in your hands?"

Oh, great. Now it was gang-up-on-Charlie-Joe time.

"Your brother is afraid of dogs!" I told Hannah. "You should know that better than anyone! He was running for his life!"

Hannah rolled her eyes. "Are you serious? He loves dogs! He practically is one!" Then she looked over at Teddy. "You told him you were scared of dogs?"

"Well, you know, what can I say?" Teddy said. Then he looked at me and grinned. "I kind of owed you one from the Camp Wockajocka basketball game." He was referring to the time at summer camp when I tricked Teddy into eating way too much pizza and throwing up all over the basketball court, which helped my camp beat his camp at basketball. I have to say, that was one of my proudest moments.

This, however, was not. This was the *opposite* of one of my proudest moments. I couldn't believe it. Teddy had made up the whole thing about being afraid of dogs! I felt my ears start to burn. It was bad enough that people were mad at me for ruining Jake's books (which used to be mine, did I mention that?). But now, Teddy had actually played a perfect practical joke on me.

That's supposed to be my job!

Without thinking, I charged Teddy Spivero. "I HATE YOU!" I shouted, and before I knew it, I was on top of him, and we were rolling around on the ground, pulling and yanking and yelling (but not punching). The whole thing lasted six seconds at the most, before various kids and adults pulled us apart.

"What's your problem!" he yelled.

"You're my problem!" I yelled back.

We were both panting like we'd just run a marathon.

"Can't you take a joke?" Teddy hissed. "How many times have you played jokes on other people? But one time someone gets you good, and you totally freak out? Are you serious?"

My parents came running over to find out what the heck was going on. When my mom saw me, she looked beyond  disappointed—she looked crushed. They pulled me off to the side so no one could hear us.

"Mom! Dad!" I said. "It's not like it looks! Teddy totally played a trick on me and we ended up in the pool drowning the Mark Twain books that you guys got me for my sixth birthday!"

"What it looks like to me," said my dad, "is you disrupting a perfectly nice party for absolutely no reason."

"Dad! They were my books!"

"But you hated them!" said my mom. "You hated reading! You still hate reading! After all these years, you still haven't changed! Everyone around you has gotten more mature, more responsible, but you're still the same old Charlie Joe!"

"Teddy hasn't changed, either," I said, lamely, looking over at him. Mrs. Spivero was giving him a lecture. He looked back at me, and we both knew we were in the same boat.

And the boat was sinking.

"This isn't about Teddy," said my dad. "This is about you figuring out how to stop acting so immature."

"That's the problem!" I said, loud enough so that heads turned in our direction. "I'm not a grown-up, so why do I have to act grown up?"

And with that, I turned and ran past the house, into the driveway and out to our car, where I decided to wait until my parents were finally ready to drive me home.

It turned out they weren't ready for a while.

After five minutes, Katie came out to the driveway.

"What's going on?" she asked me.

"Nothing," I answered.

Together, we waited for another few minutes, until I called the only person I thought of who could help me.

Ten minutes later, my sister Megan came to pick me up. Moose and Coco were in the back seat. Boy, was I glad to see all three of them!

"Do you want me to come with you?" Katie asked.

I smiled. "That would be awesome."

Katie texted her parents, then we got in the car. Megan didn't ask us one question, by the way. She just drove.

That's why I love my sister.

One day, when young Charlie Joe Jackson was either three or four years old—possibly three and three-quarters—his mother was reading him a book before bed. It was a story about a little bird that fell out of a nest, and then went all over the neighborhood asking people and things if they were his mother.

It was Charlie Joe's favorite story, and he asked his mother to read it over and over again.

Finally, after about seventeen times through the book, Mrs. Jackson was tired.

"Charlie Joe, I have to do some other things," she said. "I can't read to you anymore."

"No!" protested Charlie Joe.

"I will read to you later," his mother promised. "But maybe we should try a different story?"

"No!" announced Charlie Joe. "Same story!"

Charlie Joe waited patiently for his mother to finish the other things she had to do. He waited. And he waited. And he waited.

Finally, he realized that his mother wasn't ever coming back.

"MOM!!!" he yelled. But his mother didn't hear him.

Instead, his sister, Megan, came running into the room. "What are you yelling about?" she asked.

"Mom said she was coming back, but then she left and never came back!"

"That was only five minutes ago," Megan said.

"No it wasn't!"

"Yes it was."

"No it wasn't!"

"Yes it was!"

Charlie Joe was shocked. It had seemed a lot longer than that. But it didn't matter. He still wanted to hear his story. He started to cry.

"What's the matter?" asked his sister.

Charlie Joe was too busy crying to talk. Instead, he just pointed at the book.

"You want me to read the book to you?" asked his sister.

Charlie Joe nodded.

Megan, who was still very young herself, took a deep breath. She wasn't sure if she could read the whole thing to her little brother. It seemed kind of long, and she had never done anything like that before.

But she looked at his sad face and picked up the book.

"Are you ready?" Megan asked her brother.

He wiped away the last tear, smiled, and said, "I'm ready."

She opened to the first page.

"A mother bird sat on her egg," Megan read out loud, carefully. "The egg jumped . . ."

After the first few pages, Charlie Joe put his head on his sister's shoulder.

By the time his mom came back into the room, Charlie Joe was fast asleep.

Part Two
SMACK IN THE MIDDLE
OF EVERYTHING

1:10 pm

We were halfway home when we decided to not go home.

"Um, Katie?" I said. "In all the excitement, which you haven't asked me about—which I really appreciate by the way—I never got a chance to eat lunch."

"Oh man, that food was so amazing," Katie added, which just made my stomach grumble even louder. "You should have tried the fried chicken."

"Not helpful," I told her.

Megan eyed me in the rearview mirror (Moose was sitting in the front seat, as usual). "So where do you guys want to go?"

"Jookie's," I said.

"The Scooper Bowl," Katie said, at exactly the same time.

Megan laughed. "Well, here's an idea. It's someone's birthday today, and he gets to do whatever he wants, so why don't we do both? We'll hit up Scooper for some burgers and shakes, and then on to Jookie's for some air hockey?"

"Sounds awesome!" My mood was improving by the second. I checked the time on my phone. "The only thing is, I have to be at the school by four, for the awards ceremony." That was the big event before graduation. It was for people who were receiving special school honors, and for some crazy reason I was on the list. I figured I was getting some sort of school spirit or class clown award. But hey, I'll take it.

My phone buzzed—it was a text from my mom: Not allowed to stay mad at you on your birthday. Do you guys want us to meet you? Where are you going?

I texted back: Quick lunch with Megan and Katie. Meet you at home in an hour.

Well, that didn't happen.

1:22 pm

The Scooper Bowl specialized in "Burgers, fries, and the most freshtabulous ice cream in Connecticut!" At least, that's what the sign on the window said. I think they invented the word *freshtabulous*, which I have to say is a pretty perfect word.

"You guys wait in the car," I said to Moose and Coco, as Megan parked behind the restaurant. They didn't look happy about it, but they understood that was part of the deal of being dogs. Overall, considering all the eat-

ing, sleeping, and playing, they still had a pretty good deal, if you ask me.

The three of us sat down in a booth, and I ordered the usual: cheeseburger with cheddar, medium fries.

"It's my birthday," I told the waiter. "Do I get a free cone or something?"

"Impressive," said the waiter, who didn't look all that

impressed. "Unfortunately, free birthday cones are only for kids ten and under." He pointed three tables over, where a bunch of toddlers were shoving ice cream everywhere but in their mouths. "They're having a birthday party, you can go join them if you want."

"Fine, I'll take a black and white shake," I said, suddenly feeling old and dumb.

"That was unnecessary," Katie said, glaring at the waiter as he walked away.

While we waited for our food, Megan let out a little giggle.

"Charlie Joe, do you remember the last time we sat at this exact table?"

I thought for a second. Megan and I got along really well, but that didn't mean we went out for ice cream very often. More like, never.

"Uh, no, why?"

"Because it was hilarious, that's why." She pointed. "I'd just read that book for you at the library, and you were freaking out because Timmy and Hannah were having ice cream together."

"Oh, snap," Katie said. "I remember hearing about that. I remember hearing about that *a lot*."

"Oh yeah, it's a little foggy but it's coming back to me now," I said, which was a complete and utter lie. I remembered every second of that day like it was yesterday.

"Watching you watch Timmy as he flirted with Hannah

was pretty hilarious," Megan said. "You looked like you wanted to take his milkshake and pour it down his pants."

"I don't remember that," I said. Again . . . lie.

The shakes came, and I downed half of mine in one gulp. I drink milkshakes really fast when I feel a little nervous. And also, when I don't feel nervous at all. And everything in between.

Katie, meanwhile, took a tiny sip. "Charlie Joe, you spent so much time liking Hannah Spivero. Like, years."

"Do we have to talk about this on my birthday?" I whined.

"You're right, Charlie Joe, that's old news," Megan said. "Let's talk about you two. So Katie, what's the deal? When do you have to decide about private school?"

"Like, in the next few weeks, I think," Katie answered.

Megan chomped on an onion ring. "That's so cool," she said. "Are you psyched about it? I mean, private school sounds kinds of awesome in a way, right? It's almost like being in college."

"I guess," Katie said. "But I would miss my friends a lot."

"Totally," Megan agreed.

"I kind of think you should totally go," I said, out of the blue.

"Huh?" said Katie.

I gulped some more shake. "I mean, why not? Everything else is changing around here. What's one more totally

65

changing thing? Out with the old, in with the new, on to the next, right?"

They both stared at me like I had two heads.

Here's why: When Katie first told me she was thinking of going to private school, I kind of freaked out a little bit.

Fine, not a little bit—a lot.

Fine, not a lot—a ton.

It was right at the time when we were realizing we liked each other, after Zoe had moved away, and I couldn't believe the timing. Going to private school isn't exactly the same as moving, but it's basically the same thing, right? It's basically out of your life, right? Anyway, I started thinking about all the ways I could make sure she wouldn't go to private school, so we could be together. One of those ways involved a cupcake-eating chicken named Cletus. It wasn't pretty.

So the fact that I was encouraging her to go to private school after all that was kind of shocking. To them, and to me.

"Are you serious?" Katie asked. "Or is this a joke? I can't tell."

"Me neither," I said.

"You're lucky it's your birthday, otherwise I'd be getting really mad right about now," Katie said, which was funny because she was sounding plenty mad already.

I raised my hands in that clueless kind of way. "What did I do? I'm just encouraging you to go away if that's what you want."

"Who said that's what I want?"

"I think I know what's going on here," Megan jumped in. "Charlie Joe, Katie is a little hurt that you aren't asking her to stay here with you." Megan shifted her gaze from me to Katie. "And sorry, Katie, but my brother is acting out, the way he always does when he gets nervous. He's obviously a little uptight about everything that's happening and graduating from middle school and going to high school, and the fact that things got weird at Jake's party, and that it's all happening on his birthday, so it's a little hard for him to think straight right now."

Megan looked at me, nodding her head as if to say, *Jump in anytime, dummy.*

"Absolutely!" I said. "You know I want you to stay! It's just, yeah, I'm not gonna lie, I am a little freaked out by everything that's going on today."

"I'm going to wait in the car with the dogs," was Katie's answer. "Happy birthday."

"Thanks," I said, but she was gone by then.

I went back to my burger, and Megan went back to her salad, and neither of us said anything.

After about five minutes, Megan slurped the last of her diet coke, then looked at me. "Life gets more complicated as you get older, huh?"

I nodded. "You're telling me," I said.

It was true. Things were so much simpler, once upon a time.

FLASHBACK!!

After the first few months of kindergarten, young Charlie Joe Jackson got over his fear of school and was already starting to establish his position as one of the most interesting characters in his class. He wasn't big on reading, that much was true, but otherwise, he was smart, lively, funny, and interested in the world around him. He'd made some friends, too: his next-door neighbor, the adorable blonde-headed boy named Timmy McGibney, who was still a little annoying but also funny and reliable; and Pete Milano, whose main claim to fame was that he shoved things up his nose that weren't all that easy to get out.

These three young boys loved recess, where they got to run around, play games, and let out all that little-boy energy that had been pent up inside them all morning in the classroom. Their favorite activity, by far, was kickball. Many boys in the grade felt the same way: and so, on most days, the softball field was filled with running, throwing, kicking, yelling, and all sorts of kickball fun.

One day, however, everything changed.

It was the middle of the game, and Charlie Joe

was pitching. He was a tricky little pitcher, rolling the ball with a wicked spin that made it hard to kick. After a strapping young boy named Phil Manning popped up to second base, he angrily kicked the ground and said, "Charlie Joe, you're not pitching fair!"

"Yes, I am," Charlie Joe said. "It's not my fault if you can't kick it."

"Nobody can kick it!" Phil responded.

Other boys started piping in. "Yeah, Charlie Joe, pitch fair! No spinning! Cut it out!"

"You guys are all a bunch of chickens!" Charlie Joe hollered back.

This typical back-and-forth went on for a few more seconds until suddenly a strange voice rang out.

"Do you guys mind if I try?" the voice said. "Charlie Joe, will you pitch to me?"

All the boys' heads turned in a single direction—toward the fence behind first base, where a girl was standing.

The girl walked over to Charlie Joe. He recognized her—her name was Katie, and she was in his class.

"I'd like to play," said Katie. "Would that be okay?"

Charlie Joe shook his head. "This is a boys'

game," he said. "Sorry." He turned around, back to his friends. "Okay, who's up?"

Charlie Joe was about to go back to the mound when Katie spoke out again.

"I'm sorry," she said. "But why is it a boys' game? Shouldn't a girl be allowed to play if she wants to?"

"What?" Charlie Joe said, dumbly.

Katie marched up to Charlie Joe. "I would like to play kickball. And if you don't let me, I may have to go tell a teacher."

Well, this was certainly a tough situation for young Charlie Joe. He hated the idea of giving in to a girl. But he certainly didn't want a teacher to tell him he couldn't play kickball anymore.

"Okay, fine," he said. "One pitch, and that's it."

"Deal," Katie said. She stuck out her hand. Charlie Joe stared at it for a second, then shook it.

"You're weird," he said to Katie.

"Thank you," she said back.

Charlie Joe turned toward his friends. "Okay, this girl wants to try and see if she can play. So she's up."

Everybody moaned and groaned.

"Just one pitch!" Charlie Joe yelled. "No sweat!"

Katie walked up to home plate. Charlie Joe stood on the mound and stared down at her. He was trying to make her nervous. It looked like it was working.

I'm going to give her my secret special super-spin pitch, *Charlie Joe thought to himself. He wound up and threw. The ball wobbled and bounced and spun its way down the dirt path to home plate. Charlie Joe waited for her to swing and miss. That would show the girls once and for all—*

THWACK!

Katie kicked a solid line drive out past third base. It rolled to a stop near the jungle gym, where a yellow-haired girl named Eliza Collins was busy telling her two best friends that she was going to be on the Disney channel one day.

Charlie Joe and his friends stood there, shocked that Katie actually kicked the ball, while she started running around the bases.

Finally, Charlie Joe screamed "Here! Here!" to Phil Manning, who was playing left field. Phil, who was by far the best athlete in the grade, picked up the ball and effortlessly threw it right to Charlie Joe, who was still standing on the mound.

By then, Katie was rounding third base and heading for home.

"Get her!" his teammates shouted, but for some reason, Charlie Joe didn't throw the ball at her, which would have gotten her out. Instead, he held on to the ball for a split second too long, and then, when he finally threw it, the ball missed Katie by two feet.

"I scored! I scored!" she squealed, jumping up and down. A bunch of her friends came over and started jumping with her.

Charlie Joe's friend Timmy came over to talk to him. "What the heck happened? You had her by a mile!"

Charlie Joe shook his head. "Uh . . ." was all he managed to say. Then he caught Katie's eye. "Can we get back to our game now?" he grumbled. "Are you satisfied?"

Katie was smiling. "Yes, you may," she said.

"Great." Charlie Joe was just about to pitch to the next batter when he noticed that Katie was still standing there. He looked up at her. She winked, then silently mouthed two words: Thank You.

"Jackson, what are you thinking

about? Snap out of it!"

I looked up. Mr. Radonski, my crazy lunatic of a gym teacher, was standing over me, two giant tubs of soda in his hand.

"These are diet, by the way," he added. Then he pointed at my milkshake. "That stuff will kill you."

"But I'll die happy," I said.

Mr. Radonski peered at my sister. "I know you," he said. "I had you in class."

"Megan," Megan said. "Charlie Joe's sister."

"You were a GREAT kid!" Mr. Radonski exclaimed. "So well behaved!" He shifted his gaze to me. "What the heck happened to you?"

I shrugged. "Just lucky, I guess."

Mr. R. took a big gulp of his drink. "Hey, Jackson, I know you have graduation later, but we're heading up to Jookie's for a little while. I'm refereeing an air hockey tournament. Why don't you come along?"

"That's where we're headed!" my sister butted in. I shot her a look. The Jookie's/air hockey part sounded fun, but the tagging along with Mr. Radonski part sounded a little less fun.

"It's my birthday today," I said, which was turning into my standard answer for everything.

"Well, why didn't you say so?!" Mr. Radonski hollered, smacking me on the back. He probably thought he was being playful, but I was pretty sure it would end up leaving a mark. "Honey, we got a birthday boy here!" Two seconds later, a woman I'd never seen before was standing at Mr. R's side, smiling down at me.

"Charlie Joe, Megan, I'd like you to meet my fiancée, Aurora," said Mr. Radonksi. "Aurora, Charlie Joe here is graduating from middle school today. And for some crazy reason, I'm going to miss his sorry butt."

I blinked, looking up at the nice, pretty, normal-looking

woman. Then I looked back at my gym teacher. "Wait a second. You're engaged? You're getting married again? To her?"

Mr. Radonski frowned. "What are you trying to say, kid? That you don't understand how someone like Aurora would want to marry someone like me?"

"No, no, of course not!" I said immediately. "I totally get it! It's more like, I, uh, just thought you liked, you know, being, you know—" I stopped talking, because there was no way I was going to finish that sentence without getting myself into more trouble.

Aurora took Mr. Radonski's hand. "Well, we all have to grow up sometime, don't we, honey?" she said sweetly.

"We sure do," he said back to her. And then they kissed.

Now I've seen everything, I said to myself.

"So what do you say?" Mr. Radonski asked. "Jookie's?"

Megan looked at me. "Your birthday, your call," she said.

"Sure, I guess, for a little while," I said.

"Let's do this!" Mr. Radonski said.

On our way out, Megan elbowed me in the ribs.

"Katie is going to be thrilled," she said.

1:56 pm

Once I convinced Katie that we'd only stay for twenty minutes, and once I kept Moose and Coco happy by giving them six French fries each, we headed over to Jookie's.

"Stop giving the dogs all that human food, they're going to get sick," Megan said. I waved her off. Make them sick? Dogs *lived* for human food.

At Jookie's we ran into our first problem at the front door.

"Wait a second," said Artie, the guy who worked there forever. He looked at Megan. "You're way too old for this place."

Megan was shocked. "Seriously?"

Artie nodded. "Oh, yeah. You have to be in middle school or below to get in here. This is a youth-friendly environment."

I laughed. "Jeez, Artie, if that's true then I can't get in, either. I'm graduating from middle school today."

I liked Artie, but he didn't have much of a sense of humor. And he was definitely a stickler for the rules.

"Nice knowin' ya then," Artie said.

My turn to be shocked. "Wait, what?"

Mr. Radonski, who was already inside, came to see what was going on. "Is there a problem, Artie?"

Artie shook his head. "No problem. Was just telling these high schoolers here that Jookie's is for youngsters."

"Great rule following!" Mr. Radonski said. "Thanks, Artie! Only, I need Charlie Joe because he's my assistant referee for the air hockey tournament."

"Well now, that's a horse of a different color," Artie said. "Go on in."

As we walked by, Artie grabbed my arm. "I was just giving you a hard time," he said. "You're still welcome here right up until you graduate."

"That's in four hours," I told him.

"Well then, you better get on with it," he said, with a twinkle in his eye. Maybe he had a sense of humor after all.

The air hockey tournament was in full swing. Kids were running all over the place, screaming their heads off, generally having a blast.

"I thought you said this was a middle school tournament," I said to Mr. Radonski.

"It is," he said. "These kids are going into sixth grade."

I couldn't believe it, and neither could Katie. They practically looked like toddlers. "No way," she said.

Mr. Radonski laughed. "Yup. Incredible how young they seem, isn't it?"

"They've probably never even heard of high school," said Megan.

Suddenly I heard a familiar voice. "CHARLIE JOE!"

I turned around and saw Timmy McGibney's little brother, Michael, running up to me. He seemed upset.

"Hey, dude!" I said. "Are you playing in this tournament?"

"I was, but this bratty kid over there said I can't play!"

"What bratty kid?"

Michael didn't answer. Instead, he took my hand and walked me over to the table, where a scrawny little kid was running around with the air hockey paddles, yelling, "Who thinks they can beat me? Who thinks they can beat me?"

I tapped him on the shoulder. "I think I can beat you."

The kid looked up at me and laughed. "Forget it, Grandpa."

"What did you just call me?"

"How old are you?" the kid said.

"Old enough that you should be afraid of me, and not calling me Grandpa!"

The kid didn't look scared at all. "Whatever," he said.

"Wow, I like this kid's nerve," Megan said.

"Reminds me of someone," Katie said.

"What's that supposed to mean?" I said, but Katie just smiled.

Michael tapped me on the shoulder. "His name is

79

Gerald, and he's the best air hockey player in our grade," he whispered.

"Oh, is that right?" I said, turning back to Gerald. "Well kid, it looks like you're about to get schooled by Grandpa."

Gerald blinked. "Wait, you really want to play me?"

"That's right."

He blinked faster. "That's not allowed. You're not in sixth grade. Unless you've stayed back, like, sixteen times."

I leaned over until my face was about four inches from his. "Watch it."

By now, a bunch of other kids had gathered around to see what was going on. Mr. Radonski came running over. "What's all this about?"

I pointed at Gerald. "It's about this little twerp here, thinking he can bully my little buddy Michael off the air hockey table, and calling me Grandpa." I grabbed one of the air hockey paddles out of Gerald's hands. "So now we're going to play a quick game."

Mr. Radonski shook his head. "Now hold on a second, Charlie Joe, you're a little bit too old—"

"Will everyone stop worrying about how old I am?" I snapped. Mr. Radonski looked a little shocked, so I took a deep breath. "Besides, it's my birthday. One quick game?"

"Fine." Mr. Radonski clapped his hands together. "Okay, listen up, we're going to put the tournament on hold for a minute while Gerald and Charlie Joe duke it out. First one to five wins."

Pretty much everyone at Jookie's was watching us by this point, and believe it or not, I started to feel a few butterflies in my stomach. *You're going against a sixth grader!* I said to myself. *Relax!*

I took a deep breath and we started playing. Two seconds into the game, I knew where his confidence came from. Thirty seconds later, I was losing, 2-0.

"Wassup, Grandpa?" Gerald crowed. "Lost your reflexes over the years?"

His classmates started a chant: "Gerald! Gerald! Gerald!" But I managed to block his next five shots, score on a couple of my specialty ricochet bouncers, and win the next three points.

"I was Jookie's air hockey tournament champion two years in a row," I told my pint-sized opponent.

"Whoop-dee-doo," he said.

"Man, I can't believe what a wise guy this kid is," I told Megan.

"I can," she said. "I've lived with one most of my life."

Soon, it was 4-4.

"Next point wins!" hollered Mr. Radonski.

I was just about to serve when Katie elbowed me in the ribs.

"Maybe, uh, go a little easy on him," she said.

I couldn't believe my ears. "Are you crazy? This little brat thinks he's God's gift to air hockey! I need to finish him off right here and now."

Katie rolled her eyes. It was her go-to move, and it got me every time. "Just . . . remember that he's a little kid," she said. "And you're not."

"So what? This is war!"

I served, and we bashed the little puck back and forth. Gerald smacked a laser that was headed right for the goal, but somehow I managed to make the save at the last second. Meanwhile I was firing away, but his incredibly quick reflexes made it seem like he knew what I was going to do before I did it. I had to admit—the kid was good. Very good.

Finally, after an incredibly long rally, I had an opening. Empty net! I could have totally smacked home the game-winner, but for some reason, I let up on the shot just a tiny bit. Maybe Katie's voice was in my head. In any case, it was all Gerald needed. He saved my shot, then ripped one of his own right past me, into my net.

Mr. Radonksi blew his whistle for three deafening seconds. "That's the game!" he announced. "Gerald wins!" He threw a Jookie's hat at me. "Nice try, kid. Here's a consolation prize."

Gerald threw his hands up in the air in a champion's pose, while all his little sixth grade friends piled on top of him. The kids were laughing, and screaming, and pounding him on the back—even little Michael McGibney, that traitor. I felt like a giant Great Dane, staring down at his playful puppies. It looked like they were having the best time ever, and part of me wished I was right in the middle of it.

"Jeez, it's like he just won the World Series of air hockey," Megan said.

"He did," I answered.

After a minute or so, Gerald came up to me. "You got

owned!" he said, strutting around in circles like a half-crazed peacock.

I was about to talk smack back to him, but I decided to be the bigger man. "I guess I did," I said. Then I put out my hand. "Good game."

Gerald looked suspicious for a second, but then he shook it. "Good game to you, too. See you around."

"Not here you won't," I said. "It turns out I'm too old for this place."

"Oh," said Gerald. "Bummer for you."

He was right about that. "Yeah, bummer for me."

Katie came up to us and grabbed Gerald's shoulders. "Kid, I got one piece of advice for you as you head into middle school," she said.

Gerald looked at her. "What's that?"

"Don't be a jerk." Then she nodded her head in my direction. "We already got enough of those in this town," she said.

2:40 pm

"Guess what?" Megan said, as we walked
to the car after the Great Jookie's Air-hockey Extra-
vaganza.

Katie and I looked at her. "What?" I said.

Megan giggled. "Now it's *my* turn to say where we're
going."

"What do you mean?" I said. "We need to go home. I
have to get ready!"

"Nope," said Megan, shaking her head. "We've still got
a little time. And I promised Willy I'd meet him at Rogers
Field to watch his brother pitch."

"Now?" Willy was Megan's boyfriend, and a really nice
guy and everything, but I had to be at the awards ceremony in under an hour and a half.

"Yup, now," said Megan. "It's the playoffs. I can't
not go."

"It's fine," Katie told me. "We'll only stay like forty-five
minutes. We can walk the dogs while Megan hangs out
with Willy."

"I'll buy you a frozen Milky Way," Megan told me. "It's

85

your birthday, though, so this is the one day of the year you can overrule me, if you want to."

I scratched Moose on the back of the ear. "I don't know." The thing is, I had mixed feelings about Rogers Field. It was the sight of some of my happiest Little League memories, but it was also where I saw Jake Katz make the catch that turned him into a hero, which was how I got the idea to set him up with Hannah, which ended up being the decision that changed everything.

Anyway, I hadn't been back to Rogers Field for two years.

I was about to say no . . . but then I remembered how Willy had helped me out a while back, when I had my one-day dog-walking business. He helped me drive all the dogs to the lake, and didn't mind at all that they slobbered and drooled all over his beloved Jeep. Willy was a good guy. And it seemed like he was really nice to my sister, and she liked him a lot.

"Okay," I said. "For a little while, I guess."

On the way there, I clipped the dogs' leashes back on, which made their tails start going a mile a minute. Leashes meant getting out of the car! Leashes meant taking a walk! To me, leashes meant two sore shoulders, but for them, leashes meant happiness.

But that was nothing. As soon as Moose and Coco saw us pull up to the baseball field, their happiness turned into complete and utter joy. Even though they hadn't been there in a long time, they could still taste all the half-eaten hot dog buns that had fallen off the bleachers, and the melted ice cream that had fallen out of cones.

"Arf! Woof! Arf!" they said. Which basically meant, "Get us out of this freakin' car before we hurt somebody!"

It was a beautiful day at the ball field, and Katie and I walked the dogs behind the outfield fence, while Megan went to find Willy. Moose found part of a hamburger bun, which annoyed Coco, but then Coco got even by spotting two pieces of roast beef that were smeared in mayonnaise. Satisfied customers all around.

We were standing behind the right fielder, who looked like every other right fielder I'd ever seen—bored, uninterested, and probably thinking about video games or math—when we heard a CRACK!

Katie and I looked up, as did the right fielder. The ball was heading straight toward him.

"Uh-oh," I told Katie. "This won't end well."

The kid shielded his eyes to protect himself from the sun, even though the sun was behind him. He ran forward two steps, then he ran backward three steps, then he ran to the left four steps, then he ran to the right one step. The last thing he did was the most sensible: He covered his head so he wouldn't get beaned.

The ball dropped about six feet in front of him. A roar went up from the crowd as the runners scurried around the bases. The poor kid picked up the ball and tried to throw it in to the second baseman. It wound up closer to the center fielder.

"Oh, no!" said Katie. She was watching as the boy covered up his face with his glove. It was possible he was crying.

"Shake it off, dude!" I hollered. "Get 'em next time!" But the kid was too embarrassed to move.

At the end of the inning, he ran into the dugout. All the other kids and most of the assistant coaches patted the kid on the shoulder, trying to make him feel better. But this other guy, who must have been the manager, didn't make the kid feel better at all. Instead, he just buzzed around like a mad hornet. Finally, I heard him say to the kid, "Get a helmet on! You're up this inning. Let's go, let's make this right! We need something out of you!"

"Did you hear that?" I asked Katie. "What a jerk."

"Unbelievable," she agreed.

"Let's go closer," I said, suddenly interested in what was going on.

We grabbed the dogs' leashes and found Megan and Willy in the stands behind home plate. The game was pretty close, but I wasn't really paying that much attention. That's because I was becoming more and more obsessed with this jerky manager. He scowled and paced like he was at war, not a Little League game. He yelled at the umpires when he thought they made a mistake, even though the umps were barely older than the players. And worst of all, he treated the good players way better than he treated the bad players.

"Who is that guy?" I asked Willy.

"Oh, that's Mr. Crabtree," he said. "Real idiot."

Katie shook her head. "Why does he get to coach?"

"Because he runs baseball in this town," Willy said. "If you want your kid to get playing time, you gotta stay on his good side."

"They're little kids!" Megan said. "That's crazy."

"Which one's your brother?" I asked Willy.

He pointed at a big kid on Mr. Crabtree's team, who was just about to start pitching. "That's my bro, Chad." Watching him warm up, I was impressed with how fast he threw. And also, how wild he was.

"Are your parents here?" I asked Willy.

"My mom's working at the concession stand, and my dad stands way out in center field, where he can be nervous in peace."

I looked, and saw a man pacing back and forth behind the fence. Meanwhile, Mr. Crabtree was standing there with his arms folded, chewing his gum a mile a minute, watching Chad warm up. Boy, talk about pressure.

"Easy does it, kid!" Willy called to his brother. "Nice and easy."

"Chad throws hard," I said.

Willy made a face. "I just hope he doesn't kill somebody."

Chad walked the first batter, and went to two balls and no strikes on the next. Meanwhile, Mr. Crabtree was getting more and more worked up: He started stalking around the dugout, and it looked like he was swearing to himself. Finally, he couldn't take it anymore.

"Throw the ball over the plate, son! Come on now!"

But sadly, easier said than done. After Chad walked the second guy, Mr. Crabtree stomped out to the mound for a meeting. Chad looked scared to death.

"This guy's a turd," I said to Willy.

He nodded. "Tell me about it."

Finally the coach went back to the dugout, and by some miracle, Chad got the next pitch over. The problem was, the kid hit it. It was a hard ground ball that went right through the third baseman's legs.

"No!" bellowed Mr. Crabtree.

Luckily, the left fielder was backing up the play. Unluckily, his throw hit the kid who was sliding into second base, and the ball bounced out to right field. Luckily, the right fielder was a different boy from the one who was out there earlier. Unluckily, he was just as clueless. The poor guy was as frozen as a statue.

"THROW THE BALL!" screamed Mr. Crabtree. "HURRY UP! THROW IT!"

The right fielder did exactly that. He threw it right to Mr. Crabtree.

"NOT TO ME!" the coach thundered. "WHAT IS WRONG WITH YOU?"

By then, all three runners had scored. The third baseman looked like he wanted to crawl into a hole, and the left and right fielders looked like they wanted the third baseman to make room in the hole for them.

"BRING IT IN!" Mr. Crabtree hollered, and everyone

on the field gathered at the mound. The coach started talking a mile a minute, but really softly. I had no idea what he was saying, but I'm pretty sure it wasn't, "Hey guys, whaddya say we forget about this whole thing and go get some ice cream?"

"I can't believe this jerk gets to coach," I said. "How is that possible?"

"Because nobody can do anything about it, that's how," Willy said glumly.

Well, that was all I needed to hear.

"Says you," I said.

"Uh-oh," said Katie.

I poked my head in the dugout. "Pssst, you guys!"

There were about three kids on the bench, all blowing bubbles with their gum and minding their own business. These were the bench-warmers, the ultra-scrubs, the kids who really, really didn't care. They looked up at me with mild curiosity.

"What's your name?" I asked the kid closest to me, who was sporting a pair of those wraparound goggles that no child should ever be forced to wear.

"Norman Beckles," he said. Of course it was.

"You want to see something funny, Norman?" I asked.

"Sure."

I pointed to a box of PowerBars that was sitting in the dugout. "Hand me two of those."

He did.

Without anyone looking, I quietly unlatched the fence that led from the bleachers to the field.

"Moose! Coco!" I whispered. "Delicious delicious!" That was my code phrase for *I've got treats*. Their ears perked up to high alert, and their tails started smacking into each other.

I led them over to the fence and unwrapped the Power-Bars. Then I threw them out onto the field—one to the third base side and one to the first base side. "Go get 'em!" I said to the dogs, who didn't need to be told twice. They tore out there so fast, no one even knew what was happening until those PowerBars were long gone.

Here's the thing about dogs, though. Once they're in a place they've never been to before, they want to explore everything about it. Back when I played, Moose and Coco had been forbidden to go onto the field, of course. That would be *wrong*.

Except for this time. This time, it just felt really, really right.

Once they'd finished scarfing down the PowerBars and started sniffing around the infield, people started realizing exactly what was happening. Mr. Crabtree, who was still lecturing his team at the mound, looked up.

"What are those animals doing on my field?" he hollered.

Oh, so now it was *his* field?

The kids on the team, meanwhile, weren't sure what to

do. At first they started shyly pointing at the dogs, but then Moose and Coco did what they always do—treat all children as playmates. So they went up to the kids on the mound and started jumping, licking, and pawing at them.

And the Little Leaguers? It was the first time I saw any of them smile all day.

By now, the parents were headed out onto the field as well. Of course, there were a couple of dads who were just like Mr. Crabtree, yelling, "This is a baseball game! What is going on here? Clear the field!" and stuff like that. But most of the parents thought it was pretty darn funny. Which made me happy. It's good to know that not every adult is a crazy sports fanatic who makes their kid miserable. It's mostly the ones in charge who do it.

"Uh, Charlie Joe?" said Willy. "You maybe want to call your dogs?"

"Not really," I said. "They've never been out onto the field before. I think they really like it."

Megan smacked me lightly on the back of the head. "You made your point," she said. "Go get the dogs."

"Fine."

By now, the dogs were playing with the right fielder who'd misplayed the fly ball earlier. It looked like he'd gotten over it, though, considering he was rolling around on the ground and laughing hysterically while Coco got on top of him and started licking the ketchup stains smeared on his shirt.

I noticed a few other dogs had decided to join the fun and snuck onto the field; it was starting to look less like a baseball game and more like a show on Animal Planet. (Have you ever checked out that channel? It's AWESOME.) Little Norman Beckles was getting happily mauled by a black Newfoundland twice his size, and a tiny dachshund was pushing a baseball all over the infield with his nose.

It killed me a little bit, but finally I went out to the field. "Moose! Coco! Come!" They heard me and came trotting over, wagging their tails in gratitude. This had been a lot more fun than they'd expected—and a Power-Bar snack to boot!

"Time to go," I said, "before they send you guys to doggie jail."

We were heading off the field when I felt a sharp tap on my shoulder. I turned around to see Mr. Crabtree staring down at me like an angry parakeet.

"Are these your dogs?"

"Uh . . ."

I was completely tongue-tied and just about to panic when Katie suddenly appeared at my side to rescue me. "Yes, they are his dogs. Aren't they cute?"

"Are you kidding?" Mr. Crabtree waved his hand. "This is a baseball field, not a kennel."

"We're leaving," Katie said.

"Yeah, we're leaving," I echoed.

"Good!" Mr. Crabtree was standing there with a smug look on his face. "And don't come back until you learn how to respect the game!"

This was no time to be a wise guy. "Yes, sir." I said, grabbing the dogs by their collars. I was walking back to the fence when I heard a voice behind me.

"How about *you* learn to respect the *kids*?"

Megan!

She was walking up to Mr. Crabtree, with Willy and his younger brother, Chad, next to her.

Mr. Crabtree looked at her in disbelief.

"What did you say to me?"

Megan wasn't about to back down. "I said, how about you learn to respect the kids? Let them have fun, like boys are supposed to do, instead of scaring them half to death!" She pointed at Chad. "You practically made my boyfriend's brother cry." Then she looked at Chad. "Sorry, buddy."

"It's okay," he said.

"This isn't a sandbox," said Mr. Crabtree. "This is competitive sports. The kids in this town have it too good—they need to toughen up a little bit, learn how to deal with a little adversity."

I felt I had to step in and say something. "You're right, sir," I said. "We do have it too good in this town. We're really lucky. But that doesn't mean you shouldn't let us be kids. Pretty soon we'll all have to face real life. I'm going to high school next year, and it's going to be hard. So while these kids are still in fourth and fifth grade, shouldn't they be allowed to have a little fun?"

"They ARE having fun!" Mr. Crabtree turned around to face a bunch of his players and their parents, who had all gathered around to listen. "Aren't you guys having fun? Aren't you?"

A few kids nodded, murmuring, "Yup" and "Sure," and one or two of the dads made their kids raise their hands. But most of them didn't say a thing.

Mr. Crabtree's face turned bright red. "Do you people know how many hours I've dedicated to this team?" He waited for an answer, but none came. "Okay, FINE! Find another freakin' coach for all I care!"

He said that last sentence so loud, it scared Coco a little bit. Which wasn't good because when Coco gets scared, she pees on the first thing she sees.

Which happened to be Mr. Crabtree's foot.

"THAT'S IT!" the coach roared. "I'M OUT OF HERE!"

He stared me down for one last second. "You're older than these boys, you're supposed to know better," he spat out. "Grow up!"

Everyone watched him as he marched into the dugout, grabbed his clipboards, his windbreaker, his whistle, and his baseball glove and headed to the parking lot.

Two minutes later, he turned around and came back to the field, because he forgot his son.

"Marcus, let's go!" Marcus, who was tall, fast, and (obviously) the best player on the team, gathered up his two gloves, his six bats, his bat bag, and his catcher's equipment and walked toward the car.

But on his way out, he stopped, bent down, and hugged Moose and Coco.

"Thanks, you guys," he said. "That was the most fun I've had on a baseball field in a long time."

3:31 pm

After Mr. Crabtree left, the umpire decided
to postpone the rest of the game until the next day. We'd
left a mess of food wrappers and plates on the field—that's
the problem with fun, it's usually messy—so Willy, Megan,
Katie, and I started cleaning up. Coco was doing her part
by polishing off any last scraps of treats lying around, but
Moose was lying down in the shade under a tree.

"That's weird," I said to Megan. "Moose is never not
interested when eating is involved."

Megan glared at me. "You need to stop feeding him so
much junk," she snapped.

"That has nothing to do with it," I snapped back.

We fought about that a lot—she was always on me for
giving the dogs human food. My philosophy was that hu-
mans live a lot longer than dogs, so how can it be bad?

"Well, it's pretty hot out," Katie said, playing peacemaker. "That was a lot of activity for a senior citizen. He
needs a break."

"Moose isn't a senior citizen," I said. If I didn't want to

think about myself getting older, I DEFINITELY didn't want to think about Moose getting older.

I was putting the last of the PowerBar wrappers into a garbage can when my phone buzzed.

It was a text from Mom: Where are you?!? I've been calling! Awards ceremony in 30 minutes!! Oops. I checked—three missed calls.

"We gotta go." I shook Willy's hand, then went to say goodbye to his little brother Chad. "Nice game," I said. "You're a good pitcher. You throw hard."

"I like your dogs," he replied. "Can they come to every game?"

* * *

On the car ride home, Katie and I stared out the window while Megan drove. Nobody said much. We were all tired, and I had a lot to think about. We'd just been to three places where I'd spent a ton of time during the last few years: The Scooper Bowl, Jookie's, and the Little League field. I felt really old at all of them. I felt a little out of place at all of them. And yeah, it still felt good to pull the occasional goofy prank with my dogs. But how much longer could I get away with that?

In other words, it was pretty much going to be all business from here on in.

I looked down and saw the Jookie's hat that Mr. Radonski

had given me, lying on the car floor. Heck, I couldn't even go to Jookie's anymore! Oh sure—you might be thinking, why would you want to keep going to Jookie's anyway? It's way too young for you! Well, that may well be, but you've never tasted their chocolate chip cookies. I would stay young forever if I could keep eating those cookies.

But no more Jookie's. No more being a kid. Time to act like a high school student. *Grow up!* Mr. Crabtree had said. And even though he was a jerk, he seemed to be saying exactly what everyone was thinking.

Even Mr. Radonski, the gym teacher who was more immature than me, was getting married!

What was happening? Why was it happening?

And most important: What could I do to stop it?

3:59 pm

Ties and me have never gotten along.

I don't even get why ties exist. Who invented ties? What were they thinking? Did that person say to themselves, "Hey, I know! I'm going to invent an article of clothing that you tie incredibly tightly around your neck for absolutely no reason? And to make things worse maybe I'll invent an incredibly hot, uncomfortable, wool jacket to go with it?"

That person should be ashamed of him- or herself.

My point is that I don't like ties. But that didn't matter. Birthday or not, I had no say in the matter. For extra special occasions, I had to wear a jacket and tie, no two ways about it.

Which is why I was scratching, pulling, yanking, and otherwise doing whatever I could to separate my skin from the collar of my shirt, when I walked into the school auditorium at exactly 3:59 p.m.—one minute before the start of the awards ceremony.

"You're going to stretch it past repair," said my mom, walking behind me and trying to slap my hand away from my shirt.

"I know. That's the whole point."

I took a look around the auditorium. All the teachers were sitting in the front, on the right side. I saw Ms. Ferrell, my guidance counselor, and Mrs. Massey, my old art teacher—by old, I mean I had her last year, and also she's actually very old.

My Spanish teacher, Señora Cohen, was talking to Mr. Radonski, which was interesting, because Mr. Radonski had once annoyed all the Spanish and French teachers by claiming that foreign languages were overrated. I believe his exact words were, "We should be teaching the rest of the world to speak American, not the other way around!" I guess on graduation day, though, all is forgiven, and we're all one big happy family.

Jake waved. "Charlie Joe, come sit over here!" He and

Nareem were saving me a seat. The good news was that they looked just as miserable in their jackets and ties as I did. The bad news was that Timmy and Pete weren't there, because they weren't getting awards. That wasn't all that surprising. What was surprising is that *I* was there.

"Where are Katie and Hannah?"

Jake shrugged. "Probably still in the parking lot, trying to figure out how to walk in heels." We all laughed and shook our heads. The person who invented high-heeled shoes was as much of a sadist as the person who invented ties.

"There's Hannah," Nareem said, pointing. She was coming down the aisle with her parents, and yup, Teddy. He saw me and grinned.

"Another swim later, birthday boy?"

I ignored him.

"Hey, that reminds me," Jake said. "Are you mad that your birthday is on the same day as graduation?"

"Well, I'm not overly thrilled about it, to tell you the truth." I checked to see if my parents were looking, and then I unbuttoned the top button of my shirt. I can only describe the feeling as similar to what a person probably feels when they're let out of jail after twenty-five years. "But I am having a separate birthday party next weekend, so we're all good there," I added. "It's gonna be at Chow's Palace." I had recently developed an obsession with Chinese food, especially spare ribs. You haven't lived until you've had Chow's spare ribs.

I was scanning the crowd, looking for Katie and her parents, when the lights dimmed and the crowd hushed. A light went up on the stage, and there was our principal, Mrs. Sleep, standing at the microphone.

"If I could have your attention, please," she said, in that deep voice that had scared the heck out of me for years. "Welcome students, faculty, parents, family, and friends. On the day when our students will soon leave us to go on to bigger and better things, we pause to stop, and reflect, and honor those among us who have accomplished a special measure of achievement. Welcome to the thirty-ninth annual Eastport Middle School Awards Ceremony!"

The program began, and the first batch of awards was handed out. Nareem won the Math Award, for solving some theorem that probably would have stumped Albert Einstein. Hannah won the School Spirit Award, which makes sense, since she was the most loved and admired student in the whole school (see, it wasn't just me). Big Phil Manning won the Sportsman Award, maybe because if they didn't give it to him, he would have picked up Mr. Radonski and tossed him into a garbage can. And Jake Katz won the Science Award, for inventing a gadget that allows you to exercise while petting your dog. Everybody had to give a little speech after they got their prize—kind of like the Academy Awards, I guess, but without the huge orchestra—but nobody said anything particularly interesting except for Celia Barbarossa, who got the Music Award and then proceeded to tell everyone that she was giving up the flute and taking up competitive wind-surfing. I think she may have even shocked her parents with that one.

As more and more prizes were handed out and the ceremony wound down, I sat there, waiting and wondering. What awards were left? What award could I possibly win? Was there some sort of Wisenheimer Award?

Mrs. Sleep came up to the podium. "And now, I'd like to introduce Ms. Reedy."

I clapped loudly. Ms. Reedy was the librarian and reading and writing tutor, so I wouldn't blame you for thinking she was my enemy. But for some reason, she wasn't. She wasn't even my frenemy. The truth was, she was one of my favorite people at school. I wondered who would get the Library Award. Maybe I would get the Anti-Library Award.

Ms. Reedy cleared her throat. "It is my honor and privilege to give out the last award of the day, on behalf of the English department and library staff here at EMS."

My heart started pounding.

"This is the Creative Writing Award, and it goes to Charlie Joe Jackson."

Wait, *WHAT?!?!*

You know how sometimes, you have this thing where you hear something, and then you kind of feel your brain start to float away, so that it's almost like you're watching everything—including yourself—from ten feet above the ground? I think they call it an "out of body experience." Well, that was what I started having, as soon as I heard my name called.

Other kids started slapping me on the back, as I pushed myself up out of my chair. My mom jumped up and gave me a big hug, while my dad kept repeating, "I knew you could do it! I knew you could do it!" I high-fived a few other people walking down the aisle, and felt my head buzzing with disbelief as I climbed the stairs to the stage.

"Stand right here next to me," Ms. Reedy instructed.

I did as I was told.

"Charlie Joe is receiving this award for a story he wrote as part of a class assignment," she went on. "Inspired by his dogs Moose and Coco, it was a lovely little adventure about two best friends, and I just thought it was the most delicious story." She looked at me and smiled. "And I know Charlie Joe does love those animals." I thought of them out in the car, snoozing away. I always wondered why they wanted to come with us so they could wait for hours in a cramped car, instead of just relaxing on the couch at home. Probably because they wanted to be with us as much as possible. Which made sense: I wanted to be with them as much as possible, too.

"And now," said Ms. Reedy, "I'd like to present this award—which is a laminated copy of the story and a small plaque—to Charlie Joe."

She handed me the plaque and the story, and hugged me. As I hugged her back, a strange thought occurred to me. I realized that it was entirely possible that as soon as the ceremony was over, I would never set foot in that room again.

"Thanks a lot," I said. "I really can't believe this. Thank you to everyone who made this possible, especially my teachers and my parents. I know it's no secret that I never liked to read very much, so to get a writing award is kind of unbelievable. And on my birthday, and on graduation day, it's all really incredible."

I paused as everyone applauded. I looked around the

room at the clapping people, and I thought of more things that would never happen again. Ms. Ferrell would never again tell me that I needed to work hard to fulfill my potential. Mr. Radonski would never again ask me to throw a ball with my left hand, even though I'm a righty. And Mrs. Sleep would never again call me into her office and cause little beads of sweat to pop out on my forehead.

Believe it or not, I was really going to miss those beads of sweat.

The next thing that came out of my mouth was a surprise to everyone, especially me.

"But to tell you the truth, I'm not sure I'm ready to graduate just yet."

The applause slowly died down, as people looked up at me curiously.

"This school is great," I went on. "The people are nice and have your best interests at heart. They want you to succeed, but they also want you to have fun. It's like, the best place in the world to be a kid."

Ms. Reedy gave me a gentle nudge and whispered, "Charlie Joe, that's lovely, but we need to close the ceremony."

"Who wants to stay here for a while?" I suddenly blurted out.

I waited, but there were no takers. "We could go . . . I don't know . . . to the gym! Let's have one last Open Gym!"

Open Gym was awesome—the school would open up the gym from 2:00 to 4:00 every Saturday during the winter for all middle school kids in town, and we'd shoot hoops, maybe a little dodgeball, and just hang out. "Open Gym! One quick game of three-on-three! Who's with me?"

"Charlie Joe, that is a very sweet idea—" Ms. Reedy began, but she was immediately interrupted.

"I'm in," a voice rang out. "I'll totally go to the gym!"

I looked out into the audience and saw Teddy Spivero standing up and waving his arms around like a maniac. "Let's go to the gym and like, never leave!"

"Not helpful," I told Teddy.

"Charlie Joe, what are you doing?" Hannah called out.

"I don't know," I said, laughing nervously. "I really don't. I just really want to play some basketball right now."

Without waiting for an answer that I knew wasn't coming anyway, I walked to the edge of the stage, jumped down, and headed up the aisle toward the exit. "Who's coming to the gym with me?"

I took five lonely steps in complete silence. Then Jake Katz, who really was a ridiculously good friend, stood up. "I'll go!" he said. Then he shot a look at his mom, who was scowling. "I'll be back in five minutes," he added.

"I'll go, too," said Hannah.

"And me," said Katie.

"And I as well," added Nareem.

"Let's go to the gym!" I shouted.

Pretty soon, about twenty kids were up out of their seats, following me out of the auditorium. We broke into a run to make sure we were out of there before our parents fully realized what was happening.

"What are people who don't like basketball going to do?" asked a nice girl named Eden Lloyd, who'd won an art award for making a life-size sculpture of an aardvark.

"I have no idea," I said. "We'll figure it out when we get there." Then a voice behind me started a chant. "East-port Mid-dle! East-port Mid-dle!" All the other kids joined in. "EAST-PORT MID-DLE! EAST-PORT MID-DLE!"

Soon we were racing down the hall to the gym. A bunch of kids were laughing, and some were singing our school song: *We are the Lions, the mighty mighty Lions, Come inside! Feel the pride!*

I looked around and couldn't believe it. My weird idea to have one last Open Gym turned out to mean something to people!

It turned out I wasn't the only one who wasn't quite ready to leave.

We arrived at the gym, and with a flourish, I put my hand on the door.

"Let's do this!" I shouted, and a cheer went up. I yanked on one of the doors.

It was locked.

"Huh?" That was weird. The gym doors were never locked.

I pulled again. Nothing.

"Let me try," said Phil Manning, the strongest kid in the school. His face turned red as he pulled, but the door wouldn't budge.

I looked down the hall and saw Johnny, one of the custodians, fixing a window. "Johnny! Can you please let us into the gym?" I called. But Johnny shook his head.

"Can't, sorry bud," he said. "Doctor's orders." He always called Mrs. Sleep "doctor," for some reason.

By now, the kids behind me were starting to get a little restless. It had been a fun little game to play, marching down to the gym to pledge our allegiance to the school, but it was beginning to dawn on people that the graduation itself was going to start in an hour and a half. And there was still a little refreshment gathering in the courtyard after the awards ceremony.

"I guess we should go back," said Jake, who knew his mother would be stampeding down the hall any second.

"No!" I said. "Let's stay here!"

"We can't stay here forever, Charlie Joe," Katie said. "You know that."

I looked down the hall. Sure enough, the parents were coming. Mrs. Sleep and Mrs. Katz were leading the way.

I desperately yanked at the door. "Come on!"

A few seconds later I felt a hand touch my shoulder. I turned around and saw Ms. Ferrell standing there. "Charlie Joe," she said, gently. "What you said, and what you're doing—it's so sweet. But life goes on. You know that. And part of life is growing up, and moving on. You're going to do great things in high school; I know it. So let's celebrate our wonderful time here at Eastport Middle, and then get ready for the next great chapter in our lives. Okay?"

I looked up at her. She'd been with me every step of the way so far—ever since kindergarten, when she was my teacher. She always had my back, even when she was mad at me for not trying hard enough in school.

"Okay," I said. "I'm ready."

The awards ceremony was done. The gym was locked.

And my days as an Eastport Middle School student were over.

4:47 pm

After the awards ceremony, and after people finished talking about my sweet but lame attempt at extending my middle school career, we all gathered in the courtyard of the school for a short reception. The best part was that I was allowed to bring the dogs.

"Moose! Coco!" I called as I ran to the car. "Let's go get some cheese and crackers!"

I knew something was wrong with Moose as soon as I opened the door to the car. Coco jumped up, the way she always does, but Moose looked up at me groggily. His eyes were only half open. And his tail wasn't thumping a mile a minute, the way it usually did.

"Buddy? Everything okay?" I scratched behind his left ear, which was his favorite spot. It usually caused him to let out a long, satisfied groan.

But this time, nothing.

"Come on Moo-moo, out of the car!" I urged him. "Let's get some fresh air." I was beginning to get a bad feeling. I looked around to see where my mom and dad were, but they were nowhere in sight.

Moose looked at me, then pushed himself up and jumped out of the car. I knew he was doing it just for me, though, because his heart wasn't in it.

As we slowly walked to the reception, I went back over the earlier part of the day in my mind. I remembered how when Moose came in to wake me up, he was a little lethargic. And then, at the baseball field, he got tired faster than usual and lay down in the shade. Of course, I didn't think much of it at the time, because Moose is a pretty old dog. But now I was realizing that Moose was trying to tell me something.

He was trying to tell me he was sick.

"Let's go get some treats," I said. He looked up at me and gave me a halfhearted wag. That's the thing about dogs. Even when they're not feeling well, all they care about is making you happy.

Coco was nudging her big brother in the ear, trying to make sure he was okay. We walked around the courtyard until we found my parents, who were standing with Megan and talking to the drama teacher, Mr. Twipple.

"Mom? Dad? I think there might be something wrong with Moose."

"Like what?" asked my dad. He bent down to take a look. "You okay, big guy?" He scratched Moose's ear. "I'm sure he'll be fine, but we'll keep an eye on him," Dad told me. "Maybe we shouldn't keep taking him everywhere, it's a lot of work for him to get in and out of the car all day long."

"And you need to stop feeding him all that gross food," Megan added. "You're not doing him any favors, you know."

"Stop saying that!" I snapped. I suddenly got a scared feeling that maybe Megan had been right all along.

"Ready for high school, Charlie Joe?" asked Mr. Twipple. "Are you going to try out for the shows? It gets pretty intense up there, you're going to really have to be on your game."

"I don't know," I answered. "I haven't really thought about it." The truth was, I *had* thought about it. In fact, I had thought about it a lot. It would be so cool to be in a high school show. The problem was, the whole idea made me nervous. Because I knew that Mr. Twipple was right—it was intense. Just like everything else about high school.

"Well, you're definitely good enough," Mr. Twipple said. "You've got the talent. Now go show them what you've got."

"I'll try."

I was figuring out how to change the subject when Katie, Hannah, and Nareem came by. Boy, was I glad to see them.

Nareem shook his head. "Charlie Joe! That was hilarious in there! Only you would have the nerve to stage a sit-in at the junior high school gym!"

"What's a sit-in?" I asked. "I just wanted to play one last game of basketball."

Before Nareem could answer, Mr. Radonski ran up and smacked me on the back. "Hard to figure you out, little man. You spent three years walking around school acting like you'd rather be anywhere else, and then when the time comes, you don't want to leave! What's that about?"

I shrugged. "I wish I knew."

"I'll tell you," my mom said. "Charlie Joe may have moaned and groaned about school, but he loved it here. He really, truly loved it here."

I thought about that for a second. "I guess that's true."

"I loved it here, too," Katie said. "I'm going to miss it a lot."

"Me, too," Hannah agreed.

"Except the soggy fish sticks," I said. "I'm not going to miss them at all."

"I can't believe you even ate those things," laughed Katie.

I licked my lips. "It was all about the tartar sauce."

And just like that, we were off and running, telling stories about the gross food, the boiling hot classrooms in the winter, the time there was the leak in the gym and the whole floor got warped, the time a mouse ran across the stage of the auditorium during a school assembly, which made everyone scream until Mrs. Sleep chased the mouse all the way to the art room, where she trapped it in an old shoe box, took it outside, and set it free in the woods behind the school while everyone cheered.

We told stories, and laughed and laughed, and suddenly it felt like things were going to be okay. Middle school was great, but high school would be great, too. And I bet the stories would end up being just as amazing.

Hannah was in the middle of telling everyone about the time her school bus got stuck in the mud during an intense rain storm, which meant all the kids had to walk back to school while it was pouring, when Moose suddenly started making this weird wheezing sound.

We all looked down. "What is it, boy?" said my dad. He looked concerned.

Moose kept wheezing. "Dad," I said, "we should take him home."

"Good idea." Moose was lying down, so my dad tried to get him to his feet. "Come on Moose, let's go. Let's go home and get some treats." But Moose wouldn't get up. His legs were trembling, and there was a little bit of drool coming out of his mouth.

My mom bent down and looked into Moose's eyes. They were glassy. "Moose isn't well," said my mom. "We need to take him in."

Tears sprung to the back of my eyes. "Take him in? What does that mean? Take him in where? I have graduation in an hour!"

"I'll go," my dad told my mom. Then he looked at me. "I need to take him to the vet, just to see what's going on. I'm sure it's nothing. I'll meet you guys back here."

"I'm coming with you," I told my dad, without even thinking about it. "I'm coming with you and Moose."

He shook his head. "Not a good idea. I don't know how long this will take. You can't miss graduation, Charlie Joe. I'm sorry. I'll be back as soon as I can."

I felt a hand on my shoulder. It was Katie, just letting me know that she was there for me, whatever I decided to do.

"No," I said. "I don't care about graduation. I'm coming with you to take care of Moose, and that's final."

Megan put her hand on my other shoulder. "Charlie Joe, I'm sorry what I said about you feeding Moose too much human food," she said. "This has nothing to do with that."

"But it might!" I said, my voice cracking a little. "It might."

My dad sighed, while my mom bent down and hugged Moose. She smiled up at me and nodded.

"Okay, Charlie Joe," she said. "Go on with Dad. Just get our dog healthy and get back here as soon as you can, okay? We need you here. Both of you."

"I will," I said, as I hugged her and Katie goodbye. "I promise."

We finally got Moose to his feet and into the car. "You'll be okay," I kept repeating. "You'll be okay."

I think I was trying to convince myself more than him.

FLASHBACK!!

After months and months of begging, pleading, whining, moaning, groaning, and occasionally whimpering, young Charlie Joe Jackson realized that the only way he was going to end up getting a dog was by asking nicely.

"Mom? Dad?" he said one day, in his sweetest, most loving voice. "I was wondering if perhaps someday we might be able to possibly get a wonderful young dog that would complete our family in a most delightful way?"

Well, he probably MEANT to say it that way. But, since he was only in kindergarten at the time, it probably came out more like, "I want a dog! NOW!!!!"

Charlie Joe's older sister, Megan, also wanted a dog, although she was much more polite about asking than Charlie Joe was. She was much more polite about everything than Charlie Joe was. Which was fine with him. Charlie Joe wasn't much interested in politeness.

What neither of the children knew, however, was that their father also wanted a dog. Mr. Jackson always had dogs when he was growing up, and had decided that it was time to take the plunge as an adult. He was ready!

It was Mrs. Jackson who was the last hold-out.

Charlie Joe loved his mother very, very much. He thought she was just about perfect. Why only "just about?" Because the only thing that she lacked was a desire to get a dog. Unlike her husband, Mrs. Jackson had not grown up with dogs. She did not consider herself a "dog person." She worried about shedding, and pee stains, and loud barking at all hours of the night.

"Who will take care of it all day long?" she said. "I will, that's who."

They all tried to argue with her, of course, but it was no use. Mainly because she was right.

Then, one day, a miracle happened. Charlie Joe was having his usual after-school bowl of cereal when his mom came into the kitchen.

"Patty Gibson called me this morning," she said. "She heard about a beautiful lab who needs a home because the man who owns him just got married, and his new wife is allergic."

Charlie Joe looked up at his mom, but didn't say anything. He didn't have to. She knew how her son felt. There wasn't anything he could say at that point that would have made a difference. It was up to her. So Charlie Joe waited. Hoped, and waited.

"I just talked to Dad on the phone," she added. "The good thing is that the dog is about two years old, and fully housebroken."

"That's good," Charlie Joe said, trying to stay cool.

His mom sat down. "The dog is going to be brought over here tonight. We'll see how it goes for a week or so, and then make a final decision. No promises, okay?"

Charlie Joe nodded. "Okay," he said, as calmly as possible, which wasn't easy, since he was screaming with excitement on the inside. "What's his name?"

"Oh jeez," said his mom. "I forgot to ask."

It took about twenty years for the next three hours to go by. Finally, at six-thirty, the doorbell rang. The whole family ran to open the door.

Charlie Joe didn't even notice the human who was standing there. All he saw was a huge yellow head staring up at him. With two huge brown eyes. And a tail the size of a baseball bat, smacking into the door frame.

"This is Moose," said the person who was standing there.

Charlie Joe bent down and scratched Moose's ear. The dog gave out a soft, happy groan. "Hey, Moose. I'm Charlie Joe. Wanna come inside and play?"

And they were off and running.

For the first few days, Moose was a little wild. He was probably pretty nervous, because he was in a new place. And when Charlie Joe's mom tried to take Moose for walks, he nearly tore her arm off because he was so strong! But after a few days, he calmed down and even started taking short naps.

Every night at dinner, the family would gather around and watch in amazement as Moose polished off his bowl in about three monster bites.

"He enjoys eating," said Charlie Joe's mom, in the understatement of the year.

Then one night, after they'd had Moose for about five days, Charlie Joe's mom tucked Charlie Joe into bed and started reading him a story, just like she did every night. It was a funny story about a skunk that smelled like roses, which made all the *other skunks make fun of him. But the rose-smelling skunk ends up becoming friends with a little girl, who saves the skunk family from being kicked out of their home, so the rose-smelling skunk ends up being a hero.*

It was one of little Charlie Joe's favorite stories.

Halfway through the story, he felt something brush up against the blanket. It was Moose, coming to say hi.

"Is Moose allowed on the bed?" Charlie Joe asked his mom. "Just for tonight?"

She nodded. "He must want to hear the story, too," she said.

"Come here, boy!" said Charlie Joe, and the big dog jumped up, put his giant paws on the pillow, and licked Charlie Joe's face with a big SLURP!

Moose slept on Charlie Joe's bed for the next nine years.

The only thing dogs hate more than finishing their dinner is going to the veterinarian.

Which is why Moose, who had been lethargic and groggy during the whole car ride, suddenly sprang to full attention when we pulled into Dr. Dixon's parking lot.

There's no way I'm going in there, he said, without having to actually say it.

"Come on, Schmoo," I said, using one of Moose's many nicknames. "This is important. We need to make you all better."

Finally, we were able to talk Moose into going inside. He started to tremble a tiny bit as soon as we walked through the door. I think I might have been trembling, too.

"Well, hello!" said Dr. Dixon, in her incredibly friendly way. The weird thing about vets is that no matter how kind they might be to your animal, or how nice or awesome they are in general, you never want to see them. Because if you're with them, that means something's wrong with your pet.

Dr. Dixon was like that. She was one of the nicest people I'd ever met. But I was sorry to see her, as usual.

"What's going on, big fella?" she said, leaning down and scratching Moose's ear. Then she tried to give him a biscuit, but he wasn't interested. "Hmmm," she said. I knew what that meant. Dogs are all about food. If they don't want to eat, you know something is really wrong.

"I'm going to take him inside for a quick look," Dr. Dixon said. "Why don't you guys stay here for just a minute?"

"Can't we go with you?" I asked.

"Not quite yet," the doctor said. "Don't want to make him too nervous."

"He's nervous without me!" I petted Moose, to calm myself down as much as him.

"Just let Dr. Dixon do her work," said my dad.

She led Moose into the next room. He went without complaint. I guess he trusted her.

For the next several minutes, I stared up at the TV that was playing in the waiting area, but I wasn't really watching it. There was one other person there, a woman sitting with a cat on her lap. The cat had one of those cone thingies around its neck, and he didn't look too happy about it. If the only thing that was wrong with Moose was that he needed a cone around his neck, I'd be the happiest person in the world.

My dad looked nervously at his watch. "We're going to be late," he muttered, mainly to himself.

Finally, the doctor came back out, without Moose. "We're going to need to do a few tests," she said. "I think it's something with his liver or his stomach." She took a beat before saying the next sentence. "I can't rule out anything at this point. With dogs this age, there are a lot of possibilities."

"Like what?" I said. I could feel my stomach start to ball up in a knot. "Like cancer? Dad?"

My dad put his hand on my shoulder. "It's okay, Charlie Joe. We don't know anything for sure yet."

Dr. Dixon looked at me, then at my dad. "It's best if we keep Moose here tonight. We should know a lot more tomorrow."

"I'm staying with him," I announced. "Moose needs me here. I'm staying."

"That's not possible," said my dad. "You have graduation."

"It is possible."

"You can't stay with Moose overnight. Isn't that right, Dr. Dixon?"

Dr. Dixon, who was writing in her pad while pretending not to eavesdrop, nodded.

I shook my head. "That's okay, I can stay with him until bedtime."

"You're not being reasonable," my dad said. I could hear the desperation starting to creep into his voice. He was going to get upset in about two seconds.

"Dad!" I looked back and forth from him to Dr. Dixon. There was no way I was going anywhere. I played the only card I had left.

"It's my birthday. I can do whatever I want on my birthday."

"You want to skip your middle school graduation?" my dad asked, his voice rising a tiny bit. "Where all your friends are? And your teachers? After winning that award? You seriously want to do that?"

I didn't even have to think for a second.

"Yes."

"Oh, for god's sake," said my dad. Then he sighed loudly and scratched the back of his head for what seemed like five minutes.

"Fine," he said at last. "I'll go call mom." He went back outside to the car, where he'd left his phone.

I looked at Dr. Dixon, who finally put her pen down.

"You must really love that dog," she said.

Part Three

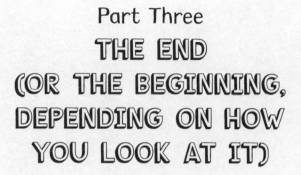

THE END
(OR THE BEGINNING,
DEPENDING ON HOW
YOU LOOK AT IT)

5:38 pm

I knew Moose was glad I was there, even though he didn't really show it.

He wasn't doing much of anything, except sleeping. He was on some kind of medicine that made him super tired. Besides, Moose slept a lot even when he was feeling great. All dogs do, especially older dogs.

But every once in a while, his eyes would open, and he would see me, and his tail would move just a little bit, and I knew he was happy I was there.

We were in a small room, with just one small light on, so it was pretty dark. My dad had left to get me something to eat, and the doctor was busy working, so I was there by myself. There wasn't a lot to do, so I went back over the whole day in my head. Jumping in the pool at Jake's house with Teddy, then driving around to The Scooper Bowl, and Jookie's, and the baseball field. And Moose and Coco were with me the whole time. They loved that, right? But maybe it was wrong. Maybe it was too much to think Moose could just be running around all day, eating French fries and PowerBars and half-eaten hot dogs. He was an old man by now. Even if he wanted to come, it wasn't a good idea.

Maybe this whole thing was my fault.

I got up to pet Moose. "I'm sorry, Schmoo," I said. "From now on I'm just going to let you snooze under the tree in the front yard and eat healthy dog biscuits. You've earned it. Think of it as a nice retirement."

He looked up at me and put his paw on my arm.

It was getting hot in there, and I realized I was still wearing my ridiculously uncomfortable dress jacket. While I was folding it (okay, throwing it) on the chair, something fell out of the inside pocket. It was the laminated copy of the story I wrote, which I'd been given as my award.

I looked at it. It was called "Moose and Bear."

"It's named after you," I told Moose.

I hadn't read it since I'd turned it in about three months earlier.

"I wonder if it's any good," I said again, also to Moose. But he wasn't listening—he was fast asleep again, snoring away.

I looked over the story—it wasn't that long. And it's not as though I had a lot of other things to do, sitting there watching my snoozing dog.

So I decided to read it.

MOOSE AND BEAR

By Charlie Joe Jackson

**

This is Moose.

This is Bear.

They're best friends.

They live in the same house.

But they're confused.

"You don't look like a Bear," said Moose.

"You don't look like a Moose," said Bear.

"Bears have growly voices," said Moose.
"Let me hear you growl."

Bear growled. Moose shook his head.

"That was not a growl," said Moose.
"That was a whisper."

Bear was insulted.

"Moose have antlers," said Bear. "Let
me see your antlers."

Moose showed Bear his antlers. Bear shook his head.

"Those aren't antlers," said Bear. "Those are furry little ears."

It was Moose's turn to get insulted.

"I don't care what you say," Moose said. "I'm a moose."

"And I don't care what you say," Bear said. "I'm a bear."

"Prove it," said Moose.

"Prove it," said Bear.

So they went outside.

Moose pointed to a tall tree.

"Bears climb trees," he said. "Climb that tree."

"Be glad to," Bear said.

She scrambled up to the first branch.

"The whole tree," Moose insisted.

"Absolutely," Bear said.

She scrambled up to a higher branch.

Then she looked down. The ground was very far away.

"I think I'm stuck," said Bear.

"Some bear you are," said Moose.

Then Bear pointed at another tree, even taller than the first tree.

"Moose eat leaves," she said. "Eat those leaves."

"Easy peasy," Moose said.

He jumped up to the first branch and ate the leaves.

"All the leaves," Bear commanded.

"Not a problem," Moose said.

He jumped up to a higher branch and ate some more leaves.

Then he looked down. The ground was very, very far away.

"I think I'm stuck, too," said Moose.

"Some moose you are," said Bear.

So there they sat.

Moose in one tree.

Bear in the other tree.

And neither one could move.

Soon, it started to get dark.

Moose and Bear were tired and scared.

Then Bear looked at Moose.

"Maybe you're not an ordinary moose,"
she called to her friend.

And Moose looked back at Bear.

"And maybe you're not an ordinary
bear," he called back.

They looked at each other.

"You're an extraordinary Moose," said
Bear.

"You're an extraordinary Bear," said
Moose.

They both thought about that for a
minute.

And they felt better.

Then, Moose lifted his head.

"I hear someone!" he said.

They looked down and saw their owner walking in the yard.

"Wow, how did you hear her?" Bear asked Moose.

"My extraordinary antlers," Moose said proudly.

Bear started yelling. "We're up here! Help! Help!"

Their owner heard Bear and stopped.

"Wow, how can you yell that loud?" Moose asked Bear.

"My extraordinarily growly voice," Bear said proudly.

Then their owner looked up and saw Bear and Moose.

"Moose! Bear!" she called. "I've been looking all over for you two! How did you get up there?"

They were too embarrassed to answer.

Their owner got a ladder and got Bear down from one tree.

Then she pulled Moose down from the other tree.

Moose and Bear hugged each other.

Then their owner hugged them both.

"Silly dogs," she said.

And Bear and Moose were more confused than ever.

THE END

5:50 pm.

"That's a pretty good story," I whispered to myself.

My phone buzzed.

A text from Dad: Mom and me on way, need anything?

I texted back: Nope. Just Moose to get better!

Dad: I know. See you in a few.

I looked down at my snoring dog. "Moose, do you sometimes wish you never grew up?" I whispered. "Are you able to remember back when you were a puppy? Do you remember when we first got you, how young and strong you were? Is it hard getting older? Is it hard growing up? Don't you wish you could have stayed young forever?" I petted him, and he stirred a little bit. "Sometimes I do," I told him. "Sometimes I wish I could stay a kid forever."

A minute later, I heard someone calling me down the hall.

"Charlie Joe?" It was my mom.

"Where are you, birthday boy?" called my dad.

I closed my eyes and sighed. I wasn't exactly in the mood to see anybody right then. Sitting there with Moose was the most relaxed I'd felt all day.

"We have a surprise for you!" called my mom.

"In here." I called back. I rubbed my eyes, got up, and opened the door.

Then I rubbed my eyes again. Not because I was tired—because I couldn't believe what I was seeing.

My parents were standing there. And behind them were about twenty kids from my class.

Timmy, Katie, Jake, Pete, Hannah, Eliza, Nareem, Phil, Celia, Mareli, Erica, Emory—the whole gang, and then some. They were all there.

My sister, Megan, was there, too, holding Coco on a leash.

I blinked a few times, as if I were seeing things. But everyone was still there.

"What—what's going on?"

My mom was smiling. "What do you mean? Last I checked, it was your birthday, and birthdays demand parties, don't they?"

"I guess," I said. I was just standing there, not moving, staring at my friends. "But—what are you guys doing here?"

"This was Katie's idea," my dad said. "She wanted to come."

"You did?" I asked her.

Katie stepped forward. "I thought all of us should

graduate as a group," she said. "We've been together for so long, we should stick together until the end, don't you think?"

"I do think." I hugged her. "But what about everybody's parents?"

"We told them we'd be back by six-fifteen," Hannah said. "They'll survive."

"Except for my mom," Jake chimed in.

Everyone laughed, as my mom emerged with a birthday cake.

"Charlie Joe," she said, "it's your birthday, but you gave me a present today."

I tried to think back. The only thing I remembered was making her mad at Jake's picnic. "I did?"

"Yes, you did," she said. "I realized something after you left with Dad for the hospital. I realized that you have grown up today. By making your own decision, by deciding to come here with Moose, and take care of him, and be with him, and by sacrificing going to your own graduation, you have shown me that you're not just a little boy anymore." She wiped away a tear. "You're a mature young man."

I noticed some of the people who worked there, including the doctors, were watching us. Even a little pug with a cast on one of its legs seemed curious.

"We're very proud of you," my dad added. "Happy birthday, son."

I took a deep breath. "Thanks, Mom. Thanks, Dad."

They hugged me, and everyone started singing. "*Happy birthday to you . . . Happy birthday to you! Happy birthday, dear Charlie Joe . . . Happy birthday to you!*"

I made a wish, took a deep breath, and blew out the candles. Everyone cheered. I felt as good as I had all day.

Then Dr. Dixon came back into the room.

5:57 pm

It's easy to say that some things are silly.

Believing in the tooth fairy is silly. Thinking there's a man on the moon is silly. Santa Claus? Not silly. There definitely IS a Santa Claus.

You know what else I used to think was silly? Thinking that wishes you made while blowing out candles on a birthday cake came true.

But that was before Dr. Dixon walked into the room at the animal hospital and said the four best words I've ever heard in my life.

"I have good news."

My mom squeezed my hand, and I heard my dad let out a huge breath of relief. "Go on," he said.

"Well, you may not believe this," said Dr. Dixon, "but labs like to eat." She paused, expecting us to laugh at her kind of lame joke, so we did. "And sometimes they eat things they're not supposed to eat." I saw my sister shoot a quick glance at me, and I immediately looked down.

Dr. Dixon went over to Moose and pretended to draw a circle on his stomach. "We caught something on an ultrasound that looks like a small plastic ring, which is clogging up his small intestine. That's why he's lost his appetite and gotten lethargic. Now, this is something that we're going to have to get out right away, so we're going to go into surgery immediately. But I expect Moose to make a full recovery. You can even visit him later tonight, if you want."

A huge cheer went up around the room. I raised my hand. "Wait, so when did Moose eat this ring? Was it, like, today?"

"Oh, definitely not," said the doctor. "Some time in the last week, I'd guess."

I wasn't done. "Could this happen from human food?"

Dr. Dixon laughed. "Absolutely not. I give my dog

human treats all the time. Not too much, of course, but every once in a while it's just fine." I felt my whole body fill with relief. "It's those garbage cans you have to look out for," added the doctor. "That's where the danger lies. But Moose will be just fine."

"YES!" I said, pumping my fist. "Moose is going to be okay!" I hugged my parents, hugged Katie, and high-fived everyone else who was there. Then I gave Moose a gentle little ear scratch, which made him groggily open one eye to see what all the craziness was about. Then he went back to sleep.

I was slapping hands with Phil Manning (which is always a painful proposition, because he has the strongest hands in the Northeastern part of the United States), when someone tapped me on the shoulder.

I turned around. "What's up, Mom?"

She tapped her watch. "We should get going."

"Get going? Where?"

She kissed me on the top of my forehead and smiled. "I believe you have someplace to be."

6:18 pm

The graduation ceremony at Eastport Middle School always takes place on the soccer field behind the parking lot, unless the weather's bad, in which case it happens in the gym. But this was a beautiful spring day, so the chairs were spread out all across the field, and the little stage was set up down by where one of the goals was supposed to be.

By the time we got there, the ceremony was already under way. The other kids and I who were late were supposed to sit up front with the rest of our class, so we took our seats as quickly and quietly as possible, while Mrs. Sleep was saying something like, "This class of students really reminded me how rewarding it is to be an educator. They are truly special."

I'm sure she says that every graduating class is "truly special," but who's counting?

Mrs. Sleep looked up and saw us come in. Then she said, "One reason this class is so special is how much they look out for each other. It looked like one of our students wouldn't be able to come to graduation because of a family emergency, and his many friends decided to join him and help him, and risk their own ability to be here. That says something about you all, and it makes me very proud." She smiled down at us, and I actually felt a warm glow inside. She paused, then adjusted her incredibly thick glasses. "And now, I'd like to introduce our special guest speaker. He is relatively new to Eastport, having moved here not long ago to be near his grandchildren, who are also in our school system. We are so honored and privileged to have him here with us today, because he has taught our young children so much with his books, which are both extremely entertaining and highly educational. Ladies and gentlemen, please welcome Mr. Ted Hauser."

A man got up from behind the stage and came up to the microphone. From where I was sitting, I could tell he looked really familiar, but at first I wasn't sure why. Then, two seconds later, it hit me. Ted Hauser was "Ted," our new neighbor I'd met earlier that day! And he was speaking at my middle-school graduation!

"Thanks to Mrs. Sleep and the entire Eastport Middle School community for having me," Ted began. "I've just moved here, but already I feel like I'm home. I remember back when . . ."

My mind started wandering, the way it often does when adults are speaking. I was thinking about the name Ted Hauser. Ted Hauser, Ted Hauser . . . Why did it sound familiar?

". . . which is why I was so struck by the young man who visited me this morning. My new neighbor, Charlie Joe."

Huh? Wha?

All eyes turned to me. I couldn't think of anything else to do, so I waved. Ted waved back.

"Charlie Joe was telling me that he couldn't wait to graduate from middle school," Ted went on. "He was so excited to start high school, and get on with his life. And I kidded around with him, saying well, not so fast, son. There's something perfect about being young. What's better than being a kid, right?" He winked at me. "But as the day went on, I thought about that conversation. And I realized, you know something? I was wrong. I'm here to tell you, there is one thing that's better than being young. And that's getting older, and growing up, and finding your place in the world, maybe starting a family of your own, and contributing to society. Do you know why that's better than being young? Because that's the journey of life. And that's the best journey in the whole world."

Ted stopped for a second, and I could hear something. It was silence. It was the silence of a hundred and eighty kids listening carefully to an adult.

That's something you don't hear very often.

"It's true, I write books for kids," Ted said. "I hope that you like them and think they're fun and funny, because to me, there's nothing better than entertaining young people." Ted was looking straight at me. "I know there are some of you out there who don't like to read very much. That's totally fine. That doesn't make you any less awesome than the other kids who do like to read. But I will say that reading is a terrific way to expand your enjoyment on this journey of life."

Ted paused for a second. "Charlie Joe, would you come up here for a quick minute?"

Oh, jeez.

I hesitated, until Katie and Timmy pushed me out of my seat. I slowly walked up to the stage, climbed up the few steps, and shook Ted's hand.

"Nice to see you again," Ted said to me.

"You, too," I mumbled.

He reached below him and pulled out a book. "Remember I said I might see you later on today, where I could give you a gift for your birthday? Well, here we are, and here you go. This is a book called *Billy's Bargain*. It's a simple little sports book, about a boy who wants to be a great pitcher. I wrote it almost twenty-five years ago, but it's still being read by kids today. That, to me, is the greatest contribution to society I could ever make." He looked out into the audience. "So Charlie Joe, and all you kids, as you think about what your own lives are going to be like, I ask you to remember this one thing: Growing up isn't just part of life." He handed me the book, then shook my hand.

"It *is* life."

The crowd starting applauding as Ted waved to the audience and said, "I signed the book for you."

I looked inside. He'd written: *Enjoy your journey. Your friend, Ted. P.S. Tell your mom the muffins were delicious.*

"I will," I told him. "Thank you."

Ted shook Mrs. Sleep's hand and sat down. As I headed back to my own seat, I stared down at the book in my hand, and slowly the whole thing started to make sense. That's why I knew the name Ted Hauser! *Billy's Bargain*! That was the book that got me in trouble . . . the book that ended my special "arrangement" with Timmy . . .

That was the book that changed everything.

By the time young Charlie Joe Jackson started middle school, he was doing very nicely indeed. He had lots of friends—even a few friends who were girls—and was well liked by both students and teachers. And he really enjoyed school, too, except for one small part.

Reading.

Charlie Joe really did not like reading at all. He found it a total waste of time. No one could convince him otherwise: Not his parents, not his teachers, not even his good friend Jake Katz, who read everything in sight.

"Some people like reading, and some people don't," Charlie Joe would say. "I'm one of those people who don't."

All this was well and good during elementary school, when the students didn't have to read all that much. But now that Charlie Joe was in middle school, not reading was beginning to become a problem. There were actual books that had to be read— and a lot of them.

One day at lunch, Charlie Joe and his friends were discussing the book that had just been assigned in English class. It was called Tuck Everlasting.

"Charlie Joe, are you going to read the book?" asked Katie Friedman, with a smile. She knew the answer—in fact, everyone did.

"Of course not," Charlie Joe responded.

"You are going to get in so much trouble," said Eliza Collins. She loved to start fights with Charlie Joe, because she had a crush on him. "The teachers are going to find out you don't do any of the reading and they're going to keep you after school."

"Fat chance," said Charlie Joe. But secretly, he was worried. He knew that he couldn't just go on not reading the books forever. He needed a plan.

Just then, Timmy McGibney came up to the table and threw his backpack down. "Hey, anybody got any money? I could really go for an ice cream sandwich, but I'm like, twenty-five cents short." Everyone shook their heads, not just to say no, but also because they were annoyed. Timmy was a total moocher.

"Dang it," Timmy said. "No one? A quarter?"

As Charlie Joe watched Timmy rifle through his backpack, looking for stray change, he suddenly had an idea.

"Hey, Timmy," he said. "I'll buy you an ice cream sandwich."

Everyone looked shocked, including Timmy. "You will?"

"Yup."

"Cool!" Timmy bounded up to Charlie Joe, with his hand out.

"Just one thing, though," Charlie Joe said. "I really, really need you to read Tuck Everlasting for me, and then tell me what it's about."

A confused look crossed Timmy's face. "Wait, what?"

"It's simple," said Charlie Joe. "I already read the inside cover and the first chapter. All you have to do is tell me what's in the rest of the book, after you read it. You're reading it anyway. So what's the big deal?"

"Don't do it, Timmy," said Eliza. "Charlie Joe is just being lazy. Don't help him out."

"You stay out of it," Charlie Joe told Eliza. He turned back to Timmy. "What do you say? We could do it for all the books." He nudged Timmy with his elbow. "Think of all the ice cream sandwiches you'll get to eat. For free!"

Timmy started scratching his elbows, the way he always did when he was thinking. No one said a word, as they waited for his answer. Charlie Joe secretly crossed his fingers under the table.

"So let me get this straight," Timmy said. "All I

have to do is tell you what's in the books that I'm reading anyway for class, and you'll buy me ice cream sandwiches?"

"Yup," Charlie Joe said.

"It's morally questionable," said Katie Friedman, "but then again, it's extremely clever."

"What does 'morally questionable' mean?" asked Pete Milano.

"It means Charlie Joe could go to jail," said Jake Katz.

Pete laughed. "I would totally come visit you."

"When are visiting hours in jail?" asked Hannah Spivero.

"Quiet, all of you!" said Charlie Joe.

They all turned their eyes back to Timmy, and waited.

Finally, after about thirty more endless seconds, Timmy stopped scratching.

"Deal," he said.

7:18 pm

Before all the kids left Eastport Middle School for the very last time—unless we come back for a visit, which everyone always says they're going to do but basically nobody ever does—we had one last assignment: to pose for a zillion pictures.

First, my parents got a family shot of the four of us, then they made me pose with pretty much every other possible combination of people: all my guy best friends (Jake, Timmy, Pete, Nareem, me); all my girl best friends (Katie, Hannah, Eliza); all of us together; all my favorite teachers (Ms. Ferrell, Mr. Radonski, Mrs. Massey, Mr. Twipple, Ms. Reedy, Ms. Albone); all my favorite school staff people (Rose, Johnny, Charles, Betty); and of course, a picture of just myself and Mrs. Sleep.

After we took the picture, Mrs. Sleep turned to me and said, "I would like a copy of that picture."

I looked up—way up—at her. "Why?"

She laughed her low, deep laugh. "Because students like you don't come along every day, that's why."

I wasn't sure what to say to that.

"Say thank you," my mom said, reading my mind as usual.

"I wasn't sure if it was a compliment or not," I told her.

"Neither was I," said Mrs. Sleep.

After about twenty minutes, I'd taken just about all the pictures I could take.

"Yo," I said to Timmy, who was taking a picture with his family and his girlfriend, Erica Pope. (I still can't believe I'm using the words "Timmy" and "girlfriend" in the same sentence.)

"What's up?" he asked.

"I don't think we should leave middle school quite yet."

"NOT AGAIN!" Timmy hollered, rolling his eyes.

"Shhhh!" I said. "I'm not talking about, like, trying to open the gym or anything. Obviously, that didn't work out so well." I leaned in so various adults in the immediate neighborhood couldn't hear me. "No, I mean, we need to do one last thing for everyone to remember us by."

Timmy's eyes widened in suspicion. "Like what?"

I gestured to all the people in the courtyard. "Check it out," I said. "Look at all these people, hot, bored, and tired. They need something to perk them up."

Timmy shrugged. "Like what?"

"Ice cream sandwiches," I said. "That's what."

"And where are you going to get a hundred ice cream sandwiches?"

I didn't say anything. I just smiled.

"No way."

"A hundred and one, actually, I need to save one for Moose. He loves ice cream sandwiches."

"You're insane."

"Maybe. But it's my birthday, and people are allowed to be insane on their birthdays. Come on."

Timmy sighed, shook his head, glanced over to see if his parents were watching—they weren't, because they were busy talking to some other lacrosse parents—then followed me into the school.

We made a beeline straight for the cafeteria, where I saw my favorite lunch lady, Sheila, packing stuff up for the summer. Sheila loved her cafeteria. She was awesome, and sweet, and I was going to miss her a lot.

Right now, though, I needed to tell her something.

"Sheila? They need you outside."

She looked confused. "Seriously? Who would need me out there? There's no food service today."

"I guess someone found some hot dog buns underneath the bleachers, and they want to know if they're yours."

"That makes no sense," Sheila muttered, "but okay." That was another thing I loved about Sheila. She trusted everyone. Even me.

As soon as Sheila was gone, I sprinted into the back of the kitchen, where the freezer was. I opened it up, and sure enough, there they were: a ton of hard, icy, so-frozen-they-were-steaming, ice cream sandwiches.

"Grab a couple of boxes," I told Timmy. "Let's bring them outside."

"Are you serious?"

"I've never been more serious in my life."

I reached down to grab a few boxes myself, and immediately realized there was one problem: the boxes were so frozen, they were stuck to the side of the freezer. I pulled and pulled, but those boxes weren't going anywhere.

"Oh, great," Timmy said, looking around nervously.

"No problem. That's what pockets are for." I ripped open the boxes, grabbed as many ice cream sandwiches as I could, and stuffed them inside my pants, shirt, and jacket pockets. Timmy did the same. Altogether, I think we got out of there with about twenty-five ice cream sandwiches. Not enough to feed the whole class, of course, but enough to give a few of our closest friends a nice refreshing treat. And enough to make my poor legs *very* cold.

I was just closing up the freezer when I heard a voice behind me.

"Hungry?"

We froze, just like those ice cream sandwiches in our pockets. I knew that voice. Oh boy, did I know that voice.

"I told you!" Timmy hissed at me, which didn't help at all.

We turned around and Mrs. Sleep was standing there with sweet, trusting Sheila.

"Sorry, boys," Sheila said. "She saw me hunting around

for the hot dog buns. Can't lie to Mrs. Sleep. You know how it is."

"No, of course, Sheila," I said. "It's my fault for putting you in the middle of this."

Sheila waved off my apologies. "No worries, boys." She jerked her hand toward the principal. "It's her you gotta be worrying about. Now, can I get back to business?"

"You bet." Timmy and I scurried around the counter and over to where Mrs. Sleep stood. I could feel the ice cream sandwiches starting to soften in my pockets, probably from the sweat that was seeping out from all over my body.

"What were you boys looking for in there?" Mrs. Sleep asked.

"Nothing," Timmy started to say, but I interrupted him.

"Ice cream sandwiches." I pulled one out of my pants. It was already dripping. "We wanted to bring ice cream sandwiches out to the picture-taking party. Timmy and I have a long history with ice cream sandwiches, and it seemed like fun, but we should have asked you. I'm really sorry."

Mrs. Sleep folded her arms. "Well, Charlie Joe, I appreciate the honesty. It seems like that's one thing you've learned with us here at Eastport Middle. Possibly the only thing." She held her hands out. "Can you return the ice cream sandwiches to me please?" I think she thought we had, like, five or six. She looked pretty surprised when, between the two of us, we piled up about thirty ice cream sandwiches in front of her.

"Oh, my," said Mrs. Sleep.

I looked down. "Yeah. Like I said, I'm really sorry."

As she stared down at our stolen treasure, I had one thought: *Could I possibly be brought to the Principal's Office one last time?* That would have to be some kind of a record.

"Well, I'm going to tell you boys what I'm going to do," Mrs. Sleep announced. "I'm going to give you two options."

Uh-oh, I thought to myself. I remember the last time

she gave me two options. It was after the whole Jake-reading-my-books-for-the-position-paper thing. It didn't go well.

"Options?" Timmy asked, still looking at me with daggers in his eyes.

"The first is to write a book about how wrong it is to take something that doesn't belong to you, even if it is just ice cream sandwiches that you're bringing to your friends," Mrs. Sleep said.

Oh no! Not again!!

Then the strangest thing happened: Mrs. Sleep smiled.

"However, seeing as you are graduates of this school, as of thirty minutes ago, I'm not sure it's within my jurisdiction to suggest such an activity," Mrs. Sleep said.

"What's jurisdiction?" Timmy asked.

"Shush!" I told him. Things seemed to be turning our way, and I didn't want to ruin the moment.

"I do believe it's your birthday today, Charlie Joe," Mrs. Sleep continued, "and far be it for me to rain on anyone's parade. Therefore, I will offer you another option. And that is to invite the entire class into the cafeteria for one final event—an ice cream sandwich party!"

Timmy and I looked at each other, both thinking the same thing: *Did she just say what I think she said?*

"An ice cream sandwich party?" I asked. "For real?"

Mrs. Sleep started walking toward the kitchen. "I'd better warn Sheila," she said, over her shoulder. "Now hurry up and tell your classmates, before I change my mind."

She didn't have to tell us twice. Timmy and I raced outside and just started yelling, "ICE CREAM SANDWICH PARTY IN THE CAFETERIA! Mrs. Sleep said so! Ice cream sandwich party in the cafeteria!"

Everyone looked at us like we were crazy, until that unmistakable voice came on over the loudspeaker.

"This is Principal Sleep. Please join us for one last farewell to the graduating class, with an Ice Cream Sandwich Party in the cafeteria. Parents and siblings welcome. Please pick up your trash after you're done."

Everyone looked around in happy shock, then started sprinting toward the cafeteria. The only kid who wasn't running was Katie Friedman, who was looking at me with an odd smile on her face.

"What did you do, Charlie Joe Jackson?" she asked. "What did you do?"

I smiled back at her and shrugged.

"A high school kid never tells."

7:37 pm

So this is how it ends, in the same place it began—the same place everything happens in middle school—the cafeteria.

We were all there: Timmy, Jake, Pete, Nareem, Katie, Hannah, Eliza, Phil, Celia, Mareli, Emory, Erica, and 160 other kids, scarfing down ice cream sandwiches, telling stories, making fun of each other, gossiping, laughing, screaming, having fun, and acting like kids.

"We need to sing to Charlie Joe!" someone shouted. And it began.

Happy birthday to you!
Happy birthday to you!
Happy birthday dear Charlie Joe
Happy birthday to you!

I blew out an imaginary candle on a half-eaten ice cream sandwich, and a new song began.

How old are you now?
How old are you now?

"Old enough to finally say goodbye to this school forever, and begin my journey of life!" I yelled.

Everyone cheered as Timmy smushed the rest of the ice cream sandwich into my mouth. Or, more accurately, around my mouth.

"Eat it, birthday boy!" he hollered.

"Ew!" Katie said, laughing. "You two are so gross!"

"It's the only way to live," I told her.

She rolled her eyes, which was her classic move. "Can you at least wash your face?"

"Okay."

After I got back from the bathroom, Katie was waiting for me.

"Are you ready?" she asked.

I wasn't sure if she was asking if I was ready to get back to the party, ready for the summer, ready for high school, or ready for the rest of my life.

But it didn't matter.

"Yes," I answered.

Part Four
ONE LAST THING
BEFORE I GO

21

8:10 pm

But the day wasn't over yet.

As soon as the ice cream sandwich party was over, my parents asked me if I had any last wishes before we headed home, for my favorite birthday dinner of fried chicken, rice, applesauce, asparagus—I know, I love asparagus, it's crazy, right??—and, of course, ice cream cake.

"One," I said. "One more wish. Or should I say, one more stop."

They knew exactly what I meant.

So me, my parents, and Megan piled into the car and headed over to the animal hospital. We went inside, and there was Moose, sleeping comfortably. He'd had his operation, and so of course he was on a lot of medication, so there was no way he would wake up. But he looked peaceful, and I knew he was going to get better, and that was all that mattered.

"Should we head home?" asked my mom.

"Not yet," I said.

Megan held my hand as we went and sat down next to our dog. Then I pulled something out of my pocket that

I'd been carrying with me all day—that I hadn't told anybody about.

A book.

The Adventures of Tom Sawyer by Mark Twain.

It was a little waterlogged, but it still worked.

"Wait, what?" said Megan.

"Do my eyes deceive me?" said my dad.

"Wow," said my mom.

"It was always just a matter of time," she said.

I held up my hands. "What? It's not like I suddenly love to read or anything! I found it in my pocket! And it just so happens that Moose used to love it when mom read out loud to us when we were younger." I held up the book. "And so, I'd like to read to him for a while, before we go home, if that's okay with you."

My mom kissed me on the top of the head. "It's okay with us," she said.

My dad chuckled. "Last time you had a Mark Twain book in your hand on your birthday, it didn't go so well."

"Yeah, well, I'm different now," I said. "I've grown up a little."

My mom rolled her eyes. "Since this morning?"

I smiled. "I guess so."

We all got chairs, while I turned the light on near the dog bed that Moose was lying in, and curled up as close to him as I possibly could—just the way my mom curled up next to me and Moose, all those years ago.

Then I opened up the book.

"*TOM!*"

No answer.

"*TOM!*"

No answer.

"*What's gone with that boy, I wonder? You TOM!*"

No answer.

After I read the first few pages, I looked up at my family. "This guy reminds me of somebody," I said.

"I wonder who," said my mom.

We all laughed, and I picked up the book again.

And I kept reading.

The end.

WAIT, THERE'S MORE!

I couldn't say goodbye forever without a few last tips, right? So without further ado, may I present to you five bonus tips on life, according to yours truly, Charlie Joe Jackson.

Enjoy your journey of life. But stay young at heart forever.

Your pal,
Charlie Joe

Charlie Joe Jackson's Special Bonus Tip On Life, #1:

NEVER DRESS UP.

Fancy clothes are overrated. So are fancy shoes, jackets, pants, dress shirts, and worst of all, ties. Leave my neck alone, people! The whole thing is the complete opposite of comfort and good sense.

My goal in life is to never get strangled by an article of clothing.

Yours should be, too.

Charlie Joe Jackson's Special Bonus Tip On Life, #2:

TAKE AS MUCH AS YOU WANT.

You know how whenever you're eating dessert with adults, they never take seconds? They usually say something like, "Oh no, I'm watching my weight," or, "The days when I could eat whatever I want are long gone." Well, guess what? You're young enough to eat whatever you want—and as much of it as you want, too. So take that second dish of ice cream, that third bowl of pudding, or that fourth slice of cake.

Just don't take a single bite of tomato salad.

That would be gross.

Charlie Joe Jackson's Special Bonus Tip On Life, #3:

ALWAYS BE NICE TO YOUR TEACHERS.

Believe it or not, I loved most of my teachers. When you think about it, they serve pretty much the most important role in society—trying to figure out how to take obnoxious, annoying kids like, well, me, and turn us into productive members of society. So three cheers for all the teachers! Remember to treat them with kindness and respect!

And if you tend to drive your teachers crazy, just do what I did, and make it up to them by writing a book that says how awesome they all are.

Works every time.

Charlie Joe Jackson's Special Bonus Tip On Life, #4:

READING CAN BE FUN!

You probably just fell on the floor.

It's okay, I'll wait.

I know—shocking, right? Charlie Joe Jackson, saying reading can be fun?

Well, newsflash: It's true.

BUT . . . please note I didn't say reading IS fun . . . I said it CAN BE fun. There's a big difference—for me anyway. It turns out that I have found some books that I've enjoyed. That doesn't mean I run to the nearest park bench to spend the afternoon reading. It just means that like everything else in life, some things take some getting used to, and if you open yourself up to new ideas, you might be surprised.

So yeah, I admit it. I kind of like reading now.

Please don't tell anyone.

Charlie Joe Jackson's Special Bonus Tip On Life, #5:

IT'S OKAY TO BE SAD, BUT IT'S BETTER TO BE HAPPY.

Life is a lot of things. And sometimes, it can be a little hard. And it's totally fine to be sad, or mad, or upset, when bad things happen. But you know what? Life is also awesome. There are so many things in life that are great. So whenever you're feeling a little down, just remember, soon you'll be up again. You can even make a list of things that you love about life and keep it in your pocket, just to remind you that the sadness won't last. That's what I did. Here's my list:

CHARLIE JOE JACKSON'S
TOP TEN THINGS THAT ARE
AWESOME ABOUT LIFE

1. Family
2. Having two dogs. (That's why we have two hands—so we can pet them both at the same time)
3. Chocolate milkshakes
4. The Beatles
5. Friends
6. The moment you realize that the person you like actually likes you back
7. French fries
8. Movies
9. Making people laugh
10. Summer

P.S. You know what makes life extra double interesting? The things that are awesome and sad at the same time. There's a word for it: Bittersweet. Here's a very short list of my favorite bittersweet things:

CHARLIE JOE JACKSON'S
TOP ONE THING THAT IS
BOTH AWESOME AND SAD

1. Writing the last word on the last page in the last book of a series.

AUTHOR'S NOTE

In September 2009, when I first wrote the words "Charlie Joe Jackson's Guide To Not Reading" on a blank screen, I never in a million years dreamed it would become a six-book series. I would like to thank EVERYONE who made the series a reality. I wish I could list you all by name, but inevitably I would forget one person, and it would be a really important person, and I would feel terrible. So let me just say: It has been a joy and a privilege, and I will be forever grateful.

—T.G., January 2016

GOFISH

TOMMY GREENWALD

© Suzanne Sheridan

What did you want to be when you grew up?
I don't remember, but it probably involved chocolate.

Were you a reader or a non-reader growing up?
I was a reader. My kids still haven't forgiven me.

When did you realize you wanted to be a writer?
Who said anything about wanting to be a writer? I wanted to be a television watcher.

What's your most embarrassing childhood memory?
Ages six through thirteen.

As a young person, who did you look up to most?
Everybody. I was a pretty short kid.

What was your favorite thing about school?
Making jokes in class that made kids laugh.

What was your least favorite thing about school?
Getting in trouble for making jokes in class that made kids laugh.

What were your hobbies as a kid? What are your hobbies now?
Then: Playing with dogs. Now: Owning dogs.

What was your first job, and what was your "worst" job?
I taught archery one year at summer camp. I'd never held a bow and arrow in my life. By the end of the summer, I still hadn't.

How did you celebrate publishing your first book?
By calling my wife and attempting to speak.

Where do you write your books?
The train, the library, Barnes & Noble. Anywhere but home. Home is for television and dogs.

What is the one tip you would give to yourself in middle school?
Making the class laugh isn't necessarily the way to a teacher's heart.

What is the one tip you would give to kids currently in middle school?
Enjoy it while it lasts.

Which is better: extra sleep or extra food?
Both. Extra food, then extra sleep.

SQUARE FISH

Which is extra better: extra-long summer vacation or an extra-long massage?
There's absolutely NOTHING better than an extra-long massage.

Which is worse: extra chores or extra homework?
Ugh. I get chills just thinking about both of them. I'm going to go with extra chores, since that's a lifetime sentence.

Which is extra worse: getting up extra early in the morning or picking up extra doggie doo-doo?
Dogs can do no wrong in my book, so I'll say getting up extra early.

What challenges do you face in the writing process, and how do you overcome them?
My desire to not work. When my guilt overcomes my laziness, I write.

What's your favorite movie, and why?
Jeez, I would have to say Woody Allen's *Manhattan*, because to me it is the perfect combination of comedy and drama. And of course *The Simpsons Movie*, which is the perfect combination of comedy and more comedy.

Do you have a favorite movie star?
It's a tie between Diane Lane and Beethoven the dog.

If you were going to be cast as the lead in a movie, what would it be about, and what would your character be like?
Not sure—all I know is that I would be six feet two inches tall. They can do that in the movies, right?

What's your favorite song?
Anything by The Beatles, Simon & Garfunkel, or Elvis Costello.

What makes you laugh out loud?
Watching my dog Abby steal food from the kitchen counter. (Don't tell my wife that.)

What makes you laugh out loud?
The Daily Show.

What do you do on a rainy day?
Give thanks. An excuse not to exercise.

What's your idea of fun?
Watching my kids try their hardest at something.

What's your favorite song?
Depends on the week. This week? "I'm So Sick of You" by Cake.

Who is your favorite fictional character?
Fielding Mellish.

What was your favorite book when you were a kid? Do you have a favorite book now?
Then: *Are You My Mother?* by P. D. Eastman. Now: *Letting Go* by Philip Roth.

What's your favorite TV show or movie?
So many!! TV: *All in the Family, M*A*S*H, The Honeymooners, The Twilight Zone,* for starters. Movies: *Love and Death, Manhattan, The Shining.*

SQUARE FISH

If you were stranded on a desert island, who would you want for company?
My family, as long as there was a desert school I could send the kids to.

If you could travel anywhere in the world, where would you go and what would you do?
Africa to go on safari. Someday.

If you could travel in time, where would you go and what would you do?
Eighteenth-century Vienna, to look over Mozart's shoulder when he was nineteen and writing incredible music.

What's the best advice you have ever received about writing?
My friend and agent Michele Rubin told me to change Charlie Joe's story from a picture book idea to a middle-grade novel.

What advice do you wish someone had given you when you were younger?
Stop eating Häagen-Dazs when you turn forty.

Do you ever get writer's block?
Nope.

What do you want readers to remember about your books?
That books aren't the enemy.

What would you do if you ever stopped writing?
Feel guilty.

SQUARE FISH

What do you like best about yourself?
My family.

What do you consider to be your greatest accomplishment?
Charlie, Joe, and Jack.

What do you wish you could do better?
Sleep.

What would your readers be most surprised to learn about you?
I'm the fifth funniest person in my family.

SQUARE FISH

Havoc ensues when the prettiest girl in school gets a pimple in this humorous and heartwarming illustrated middle-grade novel about friendship and identity.

Keep reading for an excerpt.

CALISTA

"AAAAAGGHHHGHGHGHGHGHHH!"

I yell like a lunatic when I see my best friends in the whole world, Ellie and Ella, running toward me.

"AAAAAIIIIEEEEEEEE!" they scream back. We hug for about five minutes. We talk at each other for five more minutes, but none of us can hear a word anyone else is saying. People are staring, but we don't care. We're back together again, and it's great.

Then the bell rings, and the school year begins.

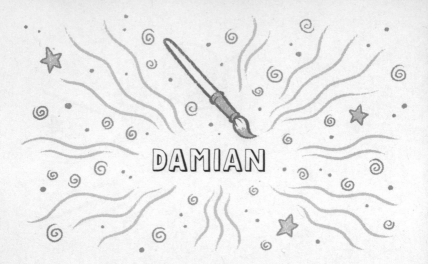

DAMIAN

I don't like it when girls yell at the top of their lungs.
It's really distracting and annoying.

So when I see three girls acting crazy, like one of them
just got back from a war or something, I walk by them
as fast as I can and go into the classroom.

It's not until I'm sitting down that I realize one of them
is Calista Getz.

CALISTA

We take our seats in first period, and I notice that two of the fluorescent light bulbs in the ceiling are flickering. Seriously? On the first day of school? No wonder the teachers are always complaining about budget cuts.

"I can't believe you're sitting next to Patrick Toole," Ellie whispers from two rows away.

"Ssssshhhhh!" I say. Ellie looks wounded, so I add, "Oh, don't be so sensitive." People take everything I say and do so seriously. It's kind of ridiculous.

I glance over to my right. "Hey, Patrick."

Patrick smiles, and his white teeth practically blind me. Okay, not really, but his teeth are extremely white. Also, you could probably build a swimming pool in one of his dimples.

"Did you have a good summer?" he asks.

"It was okay, I guess." Rule number one: Never sound too excited in front of a guy.

"Cool." Patrick looks down. He's shy in front of me. Everyone is shy in front of me, except the obnoxious boys—like Patrick's friend Will Hanson, whose only goal in life is to show off in front of his friends.

"Looking super hot, Calista!" Will says, right on cue. "Like, solar system hot!"

I try to laugh, just to be nice. I do that a lot—try to make boys feel better by laughing at their jokes. The truth is, I'm a nice person, but because I'm pretty, people don't always believe it.

"Shut up, Will," Patrick says, then turns back to me. "I'm glad you had an okay summer."

"How was yours?"

"Good, thanks."

Patrick is the me of boys. He's really cute. Everyone always thinks we should become boyfriend and girlfriend, even though I barely know him. People don't care about that, though. They just think the two most good-looking kids in the grade should go out. I guess that makes sense.

"Let's get started," says our teacher, Ms. Harnick, and my conversation with Patrick is over.

For now.

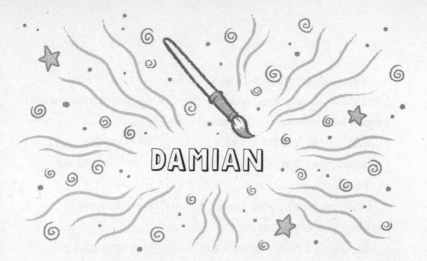

DAMIAN

"Damian White," calls Ms. Harnick.

I raise my hand. "Here."

She nods. "Welcome, Mr. White."

I put my hand down quickly. I don't like to raise my hand.

"Hey! Damian!"

I look over to my left. Will Hanson is leaning over his desk, in my direction. He has red hair and braces, and he's smiling, but not out of friendliness.

"What?"

"How was your summer?"

"It was fine."

"The weather was pretty brutal this year. So humid. That must've been tough."

I don't answer him. I feel my skin start to get sticky.

Will keeps needling me. "Do you ever take that red jacket off, by the way? What are you hiding?"

"I'm not hiding anything."

"Leave him alone," says a girl sitting behind us. I can't remember her name. She smiles at me.

Will turns around. "Hey, Laura, why don't you mind your own business? Go grab a burger or something."

The girl's eyes flash. "Real original, Will."

Will turns back to me. "Now, where were we?"

My whole back is wet.

It's a good thing I have extra shirts in my locker.

LAURA

Will Hanson is a jerk. As if I would ever let anyone like him get to me!

That's what I tell myself, anyway.

As soon as class is dismissed, the kid Will was making fun of hurries to the door. He was new last year, but I recognize him right away. He's really tall, and he always wears the same red jacket, even if it's really hot out.

As he passes my desk, he notices me and hesitates for just a second.

"Thanks," he says. "For before."

"No problem," I say, but he's gone so fast he doesn't hear me.

Read all of Charlie Joe Jackson's (mis)adventures from beginning to end!

And don't forget about his friends!